RAVES FOR TERI WOODS
AND HER NOVELS

ALIBI

"The classic investigative query—'Where were you on the night in question?'—allows Woods to once again prove why she's in a league of her own."

—*Philadelphia Tribune*

"Gritty . . . While giving a sympathetic voice to her financially desperate heroine . . . Woods observes that easy cash comes with a steep price."

—*Library Journal* (starred review)

"Woods has established herself as the Queen of Urban Fiction . . . launching a revolution in reading . . . Her hustle made real the dream of every wannabe author, the fantasy that your work will inspire a generation, will create a wave of response and thought, that posits you as a leader and a vanguard of a movement all your own."

—Heavy.com

"Street-lit queen Teri Woods moves into crime thrillers with her latest novel . . . Woods writes with feeling and a strong sense of her Philadelphia setting."

—*Booklist*

more . . .

"A fast-paced, action-filled page-turner."
—MyShelf.com

"Gritty drama that only Woods can deliver . . . [she] writes with the suspense and ingenuity of a crime novelist and has crafted a literary adrenaline rush for mystery, thriller, and urban fiction fans alike."
—The RAWSISTAZ Reviewers

"An engaging thriller with an intricate plot."
—BlackVoices.com

"A fast-paced read . . . Teri Woods is quite a good writer."
—*Sacramento Book Review*

DUTCH

"Almost unparalleled in its shock value . . . thoroughly absorbing . . . a fast-moving story with ruthless dialogue . . . which vividly highlights the crime-riddled existence of notorious Newark gangster Bernard James, aka Dutch . . . will keep any lover of this genre captivated."
—The RAWSISTAZ Reviewers

"A bone-chilling story of murder, violence, and the struggle for power. It is a harrowing tale."

—MyShelf.com

TRUE TO THE GAME III

"Vividly depicts the 1990s drug culture . . . urban fiction fans will welcome the melodramatic final entry in bestseller Woods's True to the Game trilogy."

—*Publishers Weekly*

TRUE TO THE GAME II

"Raw . . . gutsy."

—*Essence*

"Four out of five . . . Wonderful . . . a great story . . . a fast-paced, exciting read that will surely keep you on your toes."

—Urban-Reviews.com

"Explosive . . . excellent . . . masterful . . . A must-have . . . definitely worth waiting for . . . solidifies Ms. Woods's place as one of the Queens of Street Lit."

—The RAWSISTAZ Reviewers

TERI WOODS
ALIBI

GRAND CENTRAL
PUBLISHING

NEW YORK   BOSTON

Copyright © 2009 by Teri Woods
Reading Group Guide Copyright © 2009 by Hachette Book Group
Excerpt from *Alibi II* Copyright © 2009 by Teri Woods

Grand Central Publishing
Hachette Book Group
237 Park Avenue
New York, NY 10017

www.HachetteBookGroup.com

Printed in the United States of America

Originally published in hardcover by Grand Central Publishing.

First Trade Edition: June 2010
10 9 8 7 6 5 4 3 2 1

Grand Central Publishing is a division of Hachette Book Group, Inc.
The Grand Central Publishing name and logo is a trademark of Hachette Book Group, Inc.

The Library of Congress has cataloged the hardcover edition as follows:

Woods, Teri.
  Alibi / Teri Woods.—1st ed.
    p. cm.
  ISBN 978-0-446-58169-1
  1. African Americans—Fiction. 2. Robbery—Fiction. 3. Drug dealers—Fiction. 4.
  Philadelphia (Pa.)—Fiction. I. Title.
  PS3573.O6427A79 2009
  813'54—dc22   2008048145

ISBN 978-0-446-58170-7 (pbk.)

This book is dedicated to Brian Murray.

Thank you for believing in me Brian Murray, you helped me believe in myself. There would have been no hustle and no True to the Game *if not for you. Thank you for your crap money for the night. I will never forget what you did for me.*

ACKNOWLEDGMENTS

I would like to thank my family, Phyllis and Corel, Chucky, Dexter and Judy, Andrew, Christopher, Brenda and Carl, my children, Jessica, Lucas, and Brandon. I would like to thank my cousins, Lisa, Ndela, Shirley, Linda, Uncle Clarence and Aunt Vera, Louise, Debra, Sharay, LaLoni, Lori, and Ava. I would like to thank my friends, Aaron Freeman, Afriye Amerson, Aimee Minier, Alonzo Harris, Amber Ayers, Amil, Angelita DeSilva, Apalena Reynolds, Arturo of Love, Francesca Simons, Mary Ann, Bashir Cruz, Benedetta, Billy Vaughn, cousin Kim, Big Mike, Pop, Bowie, Branson Belchie, Brett Johnson, Brian Murray, Cathleen Trigg-Jones, Cavario and Khadijah, Tiffany and Kevin Chiles, Mobeys, Amy Ruths, Sylvia's, Clayton, Corey, Neet's, Sunny and Neet Viner, Mia X, DC Bookman, Devins Fish, Dion Ferron, Doug Mills, Elena George, Enjoh Palmer, Sheila Palmer, Eric, Celebrity Seafood, Farrah, Fernanda, Groovy Lou, Kendu, Rasun, Lou Hobbs, Lenise aka Queen Pen, Kashan Robinson, Jackie Rowe, Mike Tyson, Sticks, Horace Madison, J. Jesse Smith, James Ellis, Johnny Nunez and Angelique, Karen Morelli, Latoya Smith, Kenya Moore, Lamont Henchmen, Leon Blue, Manie Baron, Maria Nunez, Scott and Maria Werling, Evan and Joann Wexler, Bobby and Maria Schetilich, Mary Morrison, Meda, Melinda, Michael Coleone,

Ms. Pauline, Crystal Lacy Winslow, Miz and Oh, Monica Childs, Tracey Childs, Thomas and Betty Jones, Linda and Al Salvador, Sharwin and Nancy Green, Natasha Bynum, Nia Hill, Noble, Novella Simpson, Oouii, Pam Johnson, Pam Nelson, Portia, Raina, Richard Holland, Ricky Winkfield, Don Carlo, Councilman Oscar James, Mayor Corey Booker, Robi Reed, Sabrina Woods, STK's, Phillipe's, Crustaceans, Professor Samuel V. Jones, Saskia, Scab, Scotty, Sean Raynor, Shontay Paige, Steve Bennett, Tia, Tommy Del Gatto, Grissini's, Vella, Vic Most, and Village. To those in this industry who supported me, including but not limited to: Kedar Massenberg, Lamont Henchmen, Alan @ Koch Entertainment, Steve Rifkin @ Loud Records, Jeff Clanagan @ Code Black, Kevin Liles, Black Rob, Swizz Beats, Jada Kiss, Styles P, Sheik, Queen Pen (thank you for letting me stay with you), Amil (thank you for letting me stay with you), Jay Z, Damon Dash, Don Pooh, Remy Ma, Stevie J, Branson, Zab Judah, Keisha Cole, LL Cool J, Tyrese Gibson, Lil Kim, Hassan Johnson, Lauren London, Diamond and Arkell, Meda, Jay Ice Pick Jackson, Rocwiler, Red Man, Method Man, Des Ellis, Shauna Garr, Elle, Wendy Williams, and Hot 97. I would also like to thank all the people that give me their time, countless hours, and energy working with me. It is a pleasure to know and do business with you all, Jamie Rabb, Linda Duggins, Karen Thomas, everyone at Grand Central Publishing, Jeff Silver, Manny Haley, Joe Dinoto, Simon Rosen, Troy Carter, Tracey Braithwaite, The Portney Management Group and John Pelosi. And last but not least, a special thank you to all my favorite mom and pop bookstores, Barnes and Noble, Borders, B. Dalton, and Walden chains across the country that support me.

ALIBI

DiAnna Boston

1986

PARTY'S OVER

Hey, Lance, come here, look," whispered Jeremy, standing in an alleyway pointing to a window in what appeared to be an apartment row home on the 2500 block of Somerset Street in North Philadelphia.

"What, I don't see nothing?" whispered Lance back to him.

"The window—it's cracked. It's not shut all the way, right there. You see it?" asked Jeremy as he pointed to the window. His keen vision surpassed that of Lance, who was nearsighted and unable to see far when he wasn't wearing his glasses.

"You sure they in there?" Lance asked, trying to figure out what the next move should be as an alley cat jumped out of a tree next to him, scaring the living daylights out of him. "Nigga, I know you not laughing," he said to Jeremy, who couldn't help himself.

"You shoulda seen your face . . . Naw, for real though, I'm telling you, I followed them all day. They're in there." He shook his head, showing no signs of uncertainty in his voice. "I watched them go in there with two duffel bags. They went in and they haven't come out, neither one of them. And them duffel bags they had were chunky, real chunky. They holding a lot of money or a lot of coke. Damn, they holding."

Many different thoughts rushed around in Lance's head, the first one being how much money and how much coke their competition was holding in the house. Right now, more than ever, he needed a come up. A strong come up and he knew in his heart that this was it.

"You sure it's just the two of them in there?" Lance asked again, his heart starting to beat a little faster as the adrenaline rushed through his veins.

"Man, I'm telling you. We can take these jokers. They caught off guard. They won't even see us coming. We got one chance, Lance, just one, and this is it."

Lance needed to play the whole scene out in his head. He wanted no stone to be left unturned. There could be no mistakes, no mishaps, no fuck-ups. Jeremy might be right—this just might be his one and only chance or better yet his golden opportunity to come up. Times were hard and the only nigga in the city moving weight was Simon Shuller. Simon Shuller had been getting money for years. Everyone knew it too. Not only was he the largest drug dealer in Philadelphia, he had to be the police as well. There was no way he could run drugs, dope, and numbers year after year and not be in jail by now. But he wasn't in jail and Simon Shuller, police or not, was the man with the golden hand in the city, the big kahuna with all the money, and those two unknown suspects inside the row home on Somerset were his runners. Truth was they could have left the door wide open, 'cause anybody crazy enough to mess with anything belonging to Simon Shuller had to be plum out of their minds.

"Man, I must be crazy listening to you," said Lance, looking at Jeremy.

"Shit, you crazy if you don't, my friend. I'm telling you, we might not ever get this chance in life again. We could sneak in, take what we came for, and sneak right back out."

Lance thought for a minute longer. *Maybe Jeremy is right, we sneak in, take what we came for, and sneak back out. How hard could that be?*

"Okay, come on, let's do the damn thing," Lance commanded, feeling nothing but heart.

"That's what I'm talking about, baby boy. Don't worry, I got this caper all figured out already. Come on, let's get the car and park it close enough to make our getaway."

Up on the fire escape, Lance looked at Jeremy, who was silently cracking the window open. He turned and waved his hand for his friend to come on. He climbed through the window and into what might once have been a bathroom. Jeremy turned again, to find Lance on the fire escape climbing through the window behind him.

"What the fuck died in this motherfucker?" whispered Lance, as a foul stench filled his nostrils.

"Shh, come on," said Jeremy as he embraced his nine-millimeter and peeked around the corner of the doorway, looking like he belonged on the force.

What the fuck do this nigga think he doing?

"Whah, why you looking at me like that?"

"Nigga, you ain't no god damn Barnaby Jones and shit. What is you doing?"

"I'm trying to make sure the coast is clear, man—let me do what I do," said Jeremy, a tad bit annoyed.

What with their whispering back and forth, neither of them heard the footsteps coming down the hallway. Not until the footsteps were right on them and the bathroom door came flying open.

"What the fuck? Y'all niggas lost?" said a tall, brown-skinned fellow, wearing a Phillies jacket and Phillies baseball cap.

At first he thought they might've been crackheads, but then he saw the shiny chrome steel and knew differently.

"Shut the fuck up, before I kill you in this motherfucker," said Jeremy, quickly maneuvering his gun and pointing it straight at his victim's head. "Come on, let's go."

Jeremy held the man on his left side, close to his body. He held his gun in his right hand up to the man's head as they began walking back down the hallway. They heard another guy call out from the living room.

"Yo, Ponch, we need more vials. You gonna have to run down to the—"

His sentence was cut short as he saw his man, Poncho, being led by Jeremy and Lance through the doorway with a gun pointed at his head.

"Don't even think about it, Shorty," said Lance, pointing his gun at the guy sitting at the table stuffing tiny vials with two hits of crack.

"What the fuck?"

"Nigga, you know what it is. Bag that shit up, put it back in the duffel bag and don't nobody got to get hurt."

The man at the table, Nard, quickly surveyed everything that was going on. *These dudes ain't wearing no masks. That can only mean one thing.* And even though Jeremy and Lance's intention wasn't to kill, just rob, Nard felt otherwise and being a true thoroughbred for Simon Shuller, he'd rather die fighting than give them niggas a dime, even if the coke wasn't his. Some things in life were just more important, and his reputation for being a "real nigga" was one of them. Nard was a youngster with mad heart, and for the dough, he had love. For the streets, he had respect, and for a principle about some bullshit, he would fight tooth and nail. He slithered his arm, without a glance, under the table. Right where he had put it earlier was a tiny .22, a piece of duct tape keeping it suspended upside down. *Mmm hmm, we gonna see now, motherfucker.* Nice and smooth and just enough to do damage, he was ready, ready to pop off. Quickly, his fingers fondled the cold steel, until his grasp was tight. Nard came from under the table so fast, no one saw it coming, not even Poncho. He shot Lance one time in the chest, the bullet piercing his heart. Lance dropped to the floor holding his chest with one hand and his gun in the other, the bullet moving inside him. He looked up at Jeremy, gasping for breath and collapsing in a red pool of blood.

"Let him go, motherfucker!" shouted Nard.

"Nard, take this, nigga. Take him. I know you can, baby boy, take him," Poncho yelled.

"Shut up, shut the fuck up," said Jeremy, now nervous, as his man was gasping for air, gurgling blood, and reaching for him to help him.

"Let him go, let him go. Let him go and I'll let you live," said Nard, meaning every word he spoke, but trying to be calm as he talked Jeremy into letting his man go.

"Nigga, give me what the fuck I came for or both you

motherfuckers is gonna die," said Jeremy, with lots of heart, pushing the gun harder into the side of Poncho's head. He looked down on the floor. Lance was dead. *Oh, my god, he killed him, he killed Lance.*

"Motherfucker, I ain't giving you shit. Let him go!" Nard yelled again.

"Take him, Nard, what the fuck is you waiting fo—"

The shot from Jeremy's gun seemed unreal at first, a mistake, a misfortune, something that wasn't suppose to be, a gap, a space, time that needed to rewind. In slow motion, so slow, Jeremy felt Poncho's body slump to the floor as Nard watched Poncho, his main man, die right in front of him. Poncho's blood, and fragments of his head, landed all over the wall and covered the entire side of the room. His blood even splattered on Nard, all this within a matter of seconds.

Instinct moved through Nard, like a thief in the night, and like lightning, the bullet from that tiny .22 pierced through Jeremy's chest and threw him back several steps, as his body began to slump against the door. His fingers unable to grasp, he dropped his gun and looked down at the blood pouring out of his body, then fell to the floor, lying on his back. He stared up at the ceiling as his body stopped breathing. Jeremy didn't even see it coming, it just happened so fast. Nard hit him with the strike of magic and poof, just like that, Jeremy was gone.

"Fuck!" yelled Nard, holding his head in his right hand, his gun still in his left. "Fuck, god damn it. Fuck you come here for, stupid-ass motherfuckers?" he yelled, angrily interrogating a dead Jeremy and a dead Lance. "Damn, what the fuck am I gonna do now?"

He surveyed the room as he talked and cursed the dead bodies around him. "Motherfuckers!" he said as he kicked a lifeless Jeremy. *What am I going to do? What the fuck?* He checked the three bodies lying on the floor for a pulse, starting with his man, Poncho.

"Damn, Ponch, man. I'm so sorry, man. I'm so sorry," he said as he felt Poncho's wrist. "I love you, man. I love you. Fuck!" He started thinking about the consequences of what had just happened. "Fucking police, man. Fuck, what am I going to do?"

He just couldn't think straight, his brain was overwhelmed, to say the least. He threw all the crack, vials, and other paraphernalia into a duffel bag that was lying under the table and left the other one, which was empty lying on the floor. He looked around the room, grabbed everything that belonged to him, tried to wipe off the table, doorknobs, and everything else he had touched in the crack spot and quickly ran out the door and down a flight of stairs.

"Hey, Nard, be careful, they shooting in the building."

He quickly turned around, his gun still in his hand, but tucked inside the front pocket of his hoodie.

"Hey, Shorty," he said as he looked at a kid standing in the vestibule. He couldn't have been more than nine, maybe ten years old. He didn't know the kid's name, but this kid knew his. "Yeah, you be careful too, kid."

He quickly brushed past him, threw his hoodie over his head, made his way out the door, and quickly walked down the street to his car.

"DaShawn, get in here! Don't you hear them shooting? Come on, boy!"

Nard looked up and saw a young black girl hanging out a

window, hollering for the same young kid that Nard had just brushed past inside the building.

"I'm coming, Ma. I'm right here."

Nard could hear the little boy as he walked away from the spot.

Please tell me this kid ain't no problem, or the window chick. Fuck, man, fuck! I need me an alibi. And where the fuck is Sticks? Simon is gonna be heated, but at least I got his coke. That's all I need to do is get at Simon. I got to get rid of this gun, too. Yeah, that's all I'll need is an alibi and I'm good.

FLASHBACK

Nard drove through the park and made his way to West Philly. Even though he hustled down North, he actually lived in Southwest Philly with his grandmom and Uncle Moe on Fifty-seventh and Hatfield Avenue. He opened the door, and as usual Moe had fallen asleep in an old recliner in the far corner of the living room. He tiptoed right past him, glancing at the clock hanging on the wall in the dining room behind an archway that separated the dining room from the living room area. Too dark. He flipped on the light switch and quickly flipped it off. *Damn, it's three-thirty in the morning,* he thought to himself. He quietly made his way upstairs, tiptoeing by his grandmom's bedroom door. He walked down the hall to his room. He opened his closet door and put the duffel bag inside it. He sat on the bed and thought back over everything that had happened. *Where did they even come from? What the fuck was they thinking coming up in there trying to rob us like that? Fuck!* But of it all, he kept hearing Poncho over and over yelling inside his head.

"Take him, Nard, what the fuck is you waiting fo . . . what the fuck is you waiting fo . . ."

What the fuck?

He got up and shook the spirit of Poncho out of his head as he paced around the floor. His adrenaline was in overdrive and his speed had bypassed the limit the instant his .22 dropped Lance to the floor. He had committed a double murder. As it stood he had two bodies. *Why they have to come in there?* He could honestly say that had they been wearing masks, the situation might have played out completely different. But the wheels of time had already been set in motion. And he couldn't bring time back.

He picked up the phone and dialed Sticks's pager. *Wait till he finds out what happened. This shit is all his fucking fault. Had he been there on the lookout, things could have really been different. Damn it! And that god damn little boy, DaShawn, and his fucking mother hanging all out the window.*

"Take him, Nard, what the fuck is you waiting fo . . . what the fuck is you waiting fo . . ."

He saw Poncho, bright as day, right there in his grandmom's house, talking to him, gunman holding the gun to his head and all, bright as day, right there. *Man, come on, man.*

He waited for the series of beeps, dialed Sticks's number, and hung up the phone. He knew what had happened tonight was something that would haunt him for the rest of his life. He sat on the bed and began to rock back and forth. *This shit is crazy, man, what the fuck, I should have taken all them guns, not just mine. I did try to wipe down the table, but damn, I didn't do all the doorknobs, did I, or the back bedroom, and I didn't do the bathroom. Fuck, man, where the fuck is Sticks.* His nerves had him wired, murder had him high. Wasn't no way he was going to sleep. He couldn't if he wanted to anyway. He had way too much to do. He had to get that duffel bag of crack cocaine out of his grandmom's house. That was the first thing he had better do 'cause god help him if the cops ran up in there and found Simon Shuller's key of crack in a red duffel bag. Not only would his grandmom kill him, but Simon Shuller himself would make sure that he ended up in a duffel bag. If there was one saying he had taken heed to, it was "Never shit where you sleep." This was the first time he had ever brought drugs into his grandmom's house, and this would be the last. Therefore, that bag had to go. The second thing was the gun. He still had it. But, in his heart of hearts, he felt he needed it and couldn't let it go. If he had a replacement killer, it wouldn't have been no questions about it, that gun would have been gone. But he lived on the Southwest side of Philadelphia, and living was at an all-time low, what with junkies, crackheads, and other rivals who were simply crabs. And crabs claw at you and they don't stop—don't mean they scratch you, but they still claw. So he couldn't afford to walk out of his house without a hammer on his person. That was just the way it was. *Okay, how am I going to do this?* He had to have a plan, he needed to be strategic.

Out of nowhere, the ringing phone startled him and brought him out of his reverie. He answered on the first ring.

"Hello."

"Yo, what's cracking?"

"Man where the fuck is you at?"

"I got caught up out here in Germantown with my baby moms. Why, everything all right?"

"Fuck no, two guys ran up in the spot on me and Ponch and—"

"What you mean, two guys ran up in the spot?"

"Stickup boys, and Ponch, man, they . . . they killed him."

"What? Who killed him?" Sticks anxiously asked. "Wait, wait, don't say nothing else on the phone. Where you at?"

"My grandmom's."

"I'll be right there."

Sticks hung up the phone, his brain formulating a hundred and one questions in his head. *Man, can't nobody hold they own without me.*

Sticks set his oversized cell phone down on the seat and made a U-turn, making his way crosstown. He knew trouble when he heard it, and that call was a double dose of trouble all day long and running.

He stepped on the gas and within twenty minutes he was outside Nard's grandmom's house. Nard came dashing out the front door and onto the porch like a superspy, body all hunched down, looking all around, from side to side, as he ran down the porch steps and jumped in Sticks's Beemer, throwing the duffel bag into the backseat.

"You okay?" asked Sticks.

"Man, fuck no. Poncho's dead, Sticks," said Nard, sweat rolling down the side of his face.

"What the fuck happened?"

Sticks sat back and listened as he turned off the block and parked on a nearby side street. Nard told him everything he could think of, describing Jeremy and Lance to a tee, not holding back anything, and even telling him that if he had taken the shot Poncho wanted him to, Poncho might still be here.

"Listen, all demons gots to sleep, remember that. There's no regrets, no regrets. You can't blame yourself, feel me?" asked Sticks, listening to the series of unfortunate events and wondering what could have happened to him had he been there as he was supposed to have been.

"Did anyone see you?" asked Sticks, looking at Nard for the truth.

As soon as he popped the question, Nard could see the little brown-skinned boy, no more than ten, maybe eleven, interrupting his great escape with small talk. "Be careful Nard, they shooting in here." Not to mention his mother hanging out the window calling for him. "DaShawn, come on, boy, get in here! Don't you hear they shooting outside."

"Hey, you here?" asked Sticks waving his right hand in front of Nard's face. "Did anybody see you?"

"Yeah, this little kid, from down the hall. Then his mom, she saw me walking down the block."

"Fuck, that's not good. It always be them little kids, don't it? Always somewhere they asses don't belong."

"What I'm gonna do; you think the kid's a problem?"

"Man, I don't know. I'd feel better if he wasn't, you know. Shit, I'd rather be safe than sorry, feel me? That's all the coke back there?" asked Sticks, waiting to hear a drop was missing.

"Yeah, that's all of it."

It would be different if Nard was running game. But Sticks knew he wasn't. Sticks knew he was telling the truth.

"Listen, just in case it's a problem, just in case, let's get some kind of alibi straight. You need to be somewhere else altogether. Let me think . . . I might be able to take care of that. The only question is the little kid, and I can't call that 'cause I can't call what the kid may or may not say, feel me? I just know I wouldn't want to take the chance."

"Yeah, yeah, you right."

"Where's the gun, did you get rid of that shit?"

"Naw, not yet, it's right here."

"Man, that's the first thing you should have done. You're bugging. Here, give it to me and I'll get rid of it for you."

Nard looked at him like he was crazy. Dead body or not, he wanted his piece. It was tiny, but she did her job. His .22 was faithful and trustworthy. "Man, I would feel naked without a gun. You got another one I can hold?"

"Yeah, here, take mine," said Sticks, handing him a .44 magnum and taking the .22 from Nard, already knowing what he was going to do with it.

"You sure you got me on that alibi, right?" questioned Nard, still nervous.

"Man, relax, just relax. I'm gonna make some calls and I'll let you know."

Nard got out of the car and closed the door. Sticks rolled down the window and leaned over to the passenger side before driving away from the curb.

"You just worry about tying up the loose ends, you feel me?"

Detective Tommy Delgado walked into the vestibule of the apartment row home and made his way up the flight of stairs. He stopped and looked into the doorway. His first mental note was of the three dead bodies sprawled out on the floor. *Definitely a drug spot, definitely.* And then a quick survey of everything around him. He took out a pad and paper and began jotting down notes, from a duffel bag on the floor, to how many cigarette butts were in the ashtray, to an open unfinished bottle of beer, a pizza box, some old Adidas running shoes, and even the channel the television was on. He lifted the yellow police tape hanging across the doorway and stepped over the first body lying in front of him. He silently surveyed the room as his partner, Detective Merva Ross, entered the crime scene behind him.

"Wow, what happened here?" Ross asked as she looked around.

"Ask him, that guy right there—he looks like he would know," said Delgado, pointing to a dead Lance Robertson.

"Ha, ha, you're so funny," said Detective Ross, adding, "Do we got a time of death?"

"Um, they're pretty fresh, maybe twelve, no more than sixteen hours ago," said an officer as he watched Delgado writing on his memo pad.

"Detective Delgado, I think we got something."

An officer led Delgado down the hall to the bathroom and showed him the window.

"It's a window. Hey everybody, we got a window!" Delgado teased aloud.

"Yes, sir, it is, but it's opened and we found a piece of material that appears to ma—"

"It's a match, Honing, it looks like a match," another detective yelled from down the hall.

"Yeah, see, dead guy number two, he's wearing a jacket, but if you look really close, the side pocket is torn and we found fibers and the piece of his jacket that's torn, sir, was on the windowsill, which would lead us to believe that possibly he was an intruder breaking into the apartment, entering through the window. We're sending the fibers in for a positive match."

"Are you checking outside for prints?"

"Of course, but come here. Let me show you this. These guys, these two right here, muddy shoes, the same mud too. This guy has clean bottoms," said the officer, leading Delgado around the crime scene.

"Good work," Ross commented. "When will people learn to wipe their feet?"

"I hate that," said Delgado sneezing into his hand.

"It's the worst," added Ross. "Eeeww, here you go. You look like you need this," she said passing him a tissue.

"Thanks," he said as he wiped his nose and hands.

"You're welcome. You coming down with something?"

"I hope not."

"Me too. Look, if you make me sick, you owe me big. You keep your germs over there, pal. Damn, I'm so hungry."

"Pat's?" asked Delgado, not really wanting to eat, but able.

"My diet?"

"You still on that?" Delgado asked, looking at Merva and wondering how long she'd be on this infamous diet, which appeared to have her gaining weight instead of losing it.

"Hey, Detective Delgado, the shoes and the prints out back look like a match. This guy and this guy were in the backyard and it looks like they climbed this tree, came through the window, and then something happened."

"This guy has clean feet," Delgado pointed out.

"And?" Ross asked.

"That's dead guy number one. Dead guy number one has clean feet," replied Detective Honing.

"It means dead guy number one wasn't in the backyard and probably didn't climb the tree, and if these guys came in here, dead guy number one probably killed dead guy two and dead guy three, right here," replied Delgado, pointing at Jeremy Tyler.

"What if there was another shooter who killed all three of these guys, and he's still out there?" asked Ross, bursting Delgado's theory bubble.

"Yeah, maybe," said Delgado, as he began to think to himself.

"Did we scan for prints?" Ross asked.

"Yes, ma'am, we've got a lot of prints in here, a lot. But, we'll know a lot after forensics verifies a few things," answered Detective Honing.

"Wow, what a fucking mess," said Delgado as he looked at Poncho. "You know what I want to know? I really want to know what happened here, my friend, and if you could tell me, you would really make my job easier. Have you called the coroner yet?"

"No, sir, not yet, we're not done with them. Maybe another two hours, tops," replied Honing.

"I want the ballistics on the bullets. And find me a witness. Somebody around here knows something. See if you can figure out who and get them to talk, and I mean talk to everybody in this godforsaken rat hole. Check with everyone on this floor, the floor above, and the floor below. Ask around the block. Someone heard something and I know someone had to see something."

"Yes, sir, on it, sir," said the officer who had led Delgado to the window.

"You got me wanting a chicken cheese steak, real bad," said Ross.

"I told you, come on, let's go to Pat's. We'll see you guys back at headquarters. Come on," Delgado said to his partner.

"Excuse me," said Ross as she stepped over Jeremy, tagged body number three.

"You step over me every day and you don't say excuse me," said Detective Delgado jokingly.

"Stop crying and come on. It's your turn to treat."

Daisy Mae Fothergill stood at the end of the bar waiting for her pickup tray.

"Come on, Dallas, what you doing, man. I need my drinks so I can get up on outta here."

"Hey, Daisy, hold your tail feathers, you see me working," said Dallas as he laughed at her. "Go lay some eggs and shit and your tray will be ready when you done."

"I'm done laying eggs today and don't worry about what I need to do. You just worry about my tray. How's that?"

"Here, get on out of here, pussycat," said Dallas as he placed the remaining two drinks on the carrying tray for her.

" 'Bout time," she said lifting the tray over her shoulder and carrying it to her waiting table. That was Dallas's nickname for her; he always called her pussycat. And no, not what you're thinking, but because of her eyes, which were a crazy shade of green, and when her pupils were dilated, her eyes did resemble those of a cat.

"Daisy Mae, girl, you sure look good," said Felix, one of her regulars, as he slid his hand down the side of her bare back and squeezed her exposed butt cheek before letting her go.

"Mmm hmm, you always say the sweetest things," she said, being ever so polite. Felix was too cheap for her to patronize. He didn't want to tip, he didn't want to pay, but he wanted Daisy to stroke him as if he was king of the land or a czar on a throne.

"Naw, Daisy, I'm saying, you really looking good tonight.

Whadda you say, we go on in the back to one of them champagne rooms?"

"I'd say let's go, but you ain't got no money for no champagne. So, I guess I'll be going on home now," she said as she tried to walk away from the table.

"Daisy, naw, come here, girl, I'm trying to talk to you," he said, pulling her arm back and trying to rub her butt again. He was really the worst, literally. Daisy could tolerate some, but Felix made her skin crawl. He was a tiny man, short, balding, and had the worst breath and was always blowing his Newport cigarette smoke at her private area and licking his tongue at her.

Yuck!

"No, you don't need to talk to me, you need to talk to Calvin, honey. Ain't nothing I can do for you, and it's time for me to go."

Just then, Felix's buddy pulled out a wad of cash and flashed it at Daisy.

"See, I told you, baby, you know I'm gonna take care of you," said Felix as he nodded to his friend and pulled Daisy even closer. She fell into his lap.

"Hey, Calvin, Calvin," she called out as Felix groped her body, feeling up her naked breasts and trying to get his hand between her thighs. Calvin turned around and made his way over to the table they were at.

"What's the problem over here?"

"We want a private room, with Daisy," said Felix, nodding to his friend, who quickly flashed his wad of cash at Calvin.

"Well, Daisy, come on, take care of these guys. What y'all sitting over here for." Calvin quickly got the table on its feet. "Let me get y'all a room, and you know our rooms come with a bottle of our finest champagne," said Calvin, patting the stranger on his back. *He's so full of shit,* thought Daisy. *Ain't no Mumms no real champagne. He's crazy.* Calvin led them through a doorway and into a private champagne room. It had mirrors on the walls and ceilings, huge oversized red sofas, and black two-seater lounge chairs, a few end tables and a dancing pole in the middle of the floor. "And Daisy here, she's gonna give you your money's worth. You don't have to worry about that. Do they, Daisy?"

"No, Calvin, they ain't got nothing to worry about."

Calvin moved to the side as Daisy watched the stranger pay him for her adult-rated services. He turned and headed to the door, looked at her with his "you better do what you do, dammit" look on his face, and then closed the door behind him leaving her alone in the room with Felix and the stranger. Felix looked at her as he began to massage himself and then opened his mouth, stuck out his tongue, and wiggled it at her.

Lord, give me strength.

Two hours later, tired, hungry, feet all sore from walking around in four-inch stilettos, Daisy stood at the bus stop waiting for the number-two bus. *There has to be something better out here for me than this. I know there has to be. Please god send me a good man, someone to take care of me and love me. Please, I can't do this life much more.* Daisy could daydream until the cows came home, but at the end of the day, there wasn't nothing better out there for her and there wouldn't be nothing better either. She was only twenty-two years old, and her life had been hard, real hard. Nothing had ever been given to her and everything she got, she either took it or used her body to get it. Thank god she had that; a perfect body, a perfect frame. Other than that, she didn't have much. Just a two-bedroom apartment she shared with her ailing mother and a no-good boyfriend. Well, actually, he wasn't even a boyfriend, just some guy she had started seeing. Breaking her thoughts, her pager went off. It was him, her new guy, Sticks. *Ooh, I wonder if he's around, maybe he can give me a ride home so I don't have to take the bus.* She went over to a phone booth and called his car phone.

"Hello," said Daisy.

"Yo, Dais, what the fuck, man, I been calling you all day."

"Hey, Sticks, I'm just getting off work. I didn't even check my pager." She started looking through her pages. *Damn, he's been paging me since yesterday morning.*

"Man, I'm at the Honey Dipper looking for you. Where you at?"

"I'm around the corner, at the bus stop."

"Okay, stay there. I need to see you, man, right now."

Yes, no long, drawn-out bus ride tonight. And Sticks is coming with his fine ass, this is just perfect. She couldn't help thinking about the possibilities of the evening. She was just happy she had a ride home. And a ride from one of the city's most notorious and infamously ghetto fabulous street ballers, couldn't get no better than that. Sticks was every young girl's daydream. He was light-skinned, handsome, and muscular, with a nice grade of hair, not too curly, but definitely not nappy. He was one of them brothers a girl would get pregnant by just in hopes of having a baby with good hair. Sticks had a reputation for being a liar and a cheat with the ladies, but he also had a reputation for putting in work. Whatever had to be done, he'd do it, with no hesitation. The dudes that knew him and knew his résumé

stayed clear of him, and only a stranger would be stupid enough
to try Sticks and think he'd get away with it.

Sticks quickly put his 150E Class in drive and made his way
to the bus stop where Daisy was. He opened the passenger-side
door from inside the car and waited for her to get in.

"I sure am glad to see you. You just don't know, my feet is
killing me."

Fuck your feet—I got problems, Sticks thought to himself, and
he did; big, big, problems.

"You gonna rub them for me?"

Is this bitch serious? he thought to himself, looking at her, pretending to wear a smile. But he dare not say it. "Of course, baby,
of course. You know I got you, Dais. Anything you need, you
just let me know."

*Really, I ain't heard no nigga talk like him in all my life. Any-
thing I need, just let him know.* "Well, right now, all I need is a
hot bath, something to eat, and my feet rubbed down."

"Baby, come on, I'm gonna get you something to eat and we
going to the Inn of the Dove and you can take a hot bath in one
of them Jacuzzis and I'll rub on your feet."

"For real, you gonna do all that?"

"Yup, but I need you to do something for me," he said as he
thought of the unfortunate situation he had somehow managed
to get himself into, all because of Nard's dumb ass. *He should've
let them motherfuckers have the fucking coke, what the fuck? Simon
Shuller could count that shit up as a loss.* And he really felt that
serious about it. Truth was, he was supposed to be there that
night looking out. Had he been there, on his job, Jeremy and
Lance would never have made it through the bathroom window,
Poncho wouldn't be dead, and Nard wouldn't need no alibi.

And Simon Shuller wouldn't be telling him to fix the problem or else.

"So, what you need me to do."

"Well, it's like this, my man, he done got caught up in a little situation, you feel me. And right now, we got to help him out."

"Help him out, how?"

"Well, he needs someone to say that he was with them, that you saw him at the bar and he was in there with you. I just need you to tell an investigator for me that he was at the bar in the Honey Dipper and you remember him there all night. I'll pay you one thousand dollars if you can do that for me."

"One thousand dollars?" Daisy screeched.

"Make it two," said Sticks.

"Two thousand dollars? That's a lot of money, Sticks."

"Yeah, I know, I really need you to do that for me, though."

Not seeing the forest for the trees, Daisy agreed. She needed the money, bad. Two thousand dollars—she barely made that in a month working for Calvin at the Honey Dipper. All that dancing and everything else she had to do, you would think she was making good money. But she wasn't. Calvin was too greedy and too narcissistic. He thought he was the main man on top of the pimp and ho game. And truth be told, he was. He had them girls right where he wanted them, bent over. The funny thing was, he never touched the girls that worked in the club. He'd sometimes call them into his office individually and look them over as they stood naked in front of him. Everybody had to pass his "better be sweet" smell test. If he fingered you and you wasn't smelling right, he'd send you over to Dr. Nelson's office. But, no, no, no, he never touched them with his penis. Well, actually, every now and then he might be in the spirit of desiring sexual pleasure, but for the most part, his penis was a little too good for a whore to even suck on. Seriously, to him, his penis was special, so special that he wasn't passing his wiener around. And when he thought about it, he didn't understand how men slept around with a bunch of women. No, that just wasn't his style and yes, he was a pimp or at least he thought so. No, in his crazy mind, his job was to merely sit back and watch his girls get fucked and then fuck them out their money; that was Calvin Stringer.

The next morning, after a night of sexual bliss, Sticks and Daisy left the Inn of the Dove. Sticks promised her that the investigator would be calling her that day, and after she spoke to him, she'd be two thousand dollars richer. Daisy couldn't wait. She had plans, big plans for that extra two grand.

"Momma, come on, I need you to put on one of your overcoats," said Daisy as she rushed around the apartment trying to make it spiffy.

"What I want an overcoat for?"

"Because, Momma, I got this investigator man coming here and I don't want your titties hanging all out, come on. I need you to put something on."

"You don't need to worry about my titties hanging nowhere. You need to worry about yours. And an investigator; what you got an investigator coming in here for?"

"Momma, please, why you asking me so many questions?"

" 'Cause, you don't know what you doing. You just so fast, that's what's wrong with you now."

No she's not, no she's not getting ready to start with me about how I make my money.

"Messing with all these crazy men, and you talking to private investigators. It ain't nothing but trouble. You need to get your life together, Daisy Mae. You need Jesus. Jesus saves, did you know that?"

"Yes, you've told me before."

"Well, you need to let him save you. And what you got an investigator for? You looking for a missing person or something?"

"No, Momma, I'm helping out a friend. It's just a favor, that's all."

"Favor, favor, ain't no helping here if I got to talk to no investigator. What kind of mess you done got into now."

"Nothing."

"Well, then don't do it. Don't say nothing to no investigator without getting yourself a lawyer first. They got commercials now. I think you better call 'em."

"Momma, I don't need no lawyer, I ain't in no trouble. Come on, put this robe on, please."

"Mmm-hmm, I don't want to. I want to go in my room. I don't want no investigator looking at me. Next thing you know I'll be some kind of suspect and all messed up. No, sir, I'll go in my room and close my door."

Daisy's mother stood up but looked as if she was about to fall back down. Daisy grabbed her right arm, holding her up.

"You okay?" she asked.

"Okay, as okay can get, but I still don't want you getting in no trouble."

"Momma, I ain't getting in no trouble, please don't worry about me. Did you take your medication?"

"Yeah, but I been feeling a little funny. You know, just feel like I'm out of myself, like my body's over there and I'm somewhere over here looking for it. And my foot's been sleeping all day. I tried to shake it, but it still got them pins and needle feeling in it."

"Don't worry, when I'm done with the investigator, I'll come in and rub you down."

"Yeah, you good at them massages. At least you good for something. Now, that you can do," said Daisy's mother as Daisy helped her sit on the edge of the bed. "You just be careful, Daisy. Just be careful, baby."

"I will, Momma, I will."

Just then the buzzer to the downstairs intercom rang. Daisy closed the door behind her mother, spoke into the intercom, and buzzed in the investigator. To her surprise it was all quite simple. The investigator simply showed her a photo of Nard and asked was she sure he was in the bar with her. She answered yes, gave him a simple time frame, and signed a witness statement. That was it. After he left, she paged Sticks, and sure enough, within twenty minutes he was downstairs sitting in front of her building in his green E Class. He counted out two thousand dollars, handed it to her, and told her he'd call her later. Daisy couldn't believe it. It was like somebody else had been blessed and passed it on to her.

She thanked Sticks and hurried back upstairs. She opened the apartment door.

"Momma, it's me," she yelled out and then went into her room. She closed the door and counted out her money again. *Boy oh boy, the sun sure will come out tomorrow.* With two thousand dollars in her pocket you could bet your bottom dollar and hers. Daisy sat there making a mental list of all the things she could do. It didn't dawn on her that her mother hadn't responded. Daisy was too preoccupied with all that her small fortune would be doing for her—hair, nails, clothes, maybe even a new microwave and a TV for her room. Two thousand dollars was just so much money and she needed it so bad right now. It really was a blessing.

"Momma, guess what?" said Daisy as she made her way down the hall. "I'm gonna get you something special, Momma. You hear me?" she asked as she flung open her mother's bedroom door.

"Momma, you okay?" she asked as she walked over to the bed. "Oh, Momma, no."

Her mother was lying still, her mouth open, her eyes open, and her face wearing a look of shock.

"Mommy, please no, please god, no. Momma, please, you're all I got, Momma, please don't leave me." She rushed over to the side of her mother's bed. She sat on the side of the bed next to her mother's body. She closed her mother's eyes, and then kissed her open mouth. She rubbed her silver hair from her mother's face and patted her hand. She realized that she was all alone, and for the first time in her life, she felt afraid. At least, no matter how bad things got, she had her mother and the feeling of being truly loved by someone, but without her mother, there was nothing, nobody and no reason, no reason to even live. For the longest time, that was how it was, just Daisy and her mom. Ever since she was a little girl that was the only family she had to fall back on. Somewhere out there in Murfreesboro, Tennessee, she had an aunt and a cousin, but other than that, no family to tell of.

Her mother, Abigail, had been born in Murfreesboro in 1927 and was fifty-nine years old. She was the elder of two. Her sister,

Matilda, was six years younger than herself. Times were hard for her family, as for most, but the Wrights had established their land and their farm. People might not think of a cow or a mule as being as precious as a diamond or gold, but in those times, they really were valuable, and John Wright kept his shotgun handy at all times. Wasn't nobody taking his cow, his mule, his chickens, or his pig. That was all he had, and without them animals, his family would starve. Without the cow, no milk or cheese, butter or cream, and he needed his mule for plowing. The family lived in a house not yet equipped with electricity and running water. They had a well that they lowered buckets down into on a rope so they could pull the water back up from the earth. There was no bathroom, only an outhouse, no tub, just a large washbin to sit in from time to time. And of all the things he wished for, he most wished for a horse. *If I only had a horse. If I only had a horse.* His head sang that song for a long long time. Millie was all right, but if she cut short on a trip, decided she was tired or whatever else was ailing her, well then the trip would just be cut short. He couldn't get her to move. That was one thing about them mules, once they decided to stop, they stopped. Not even a rattlesnake would get a mule to flinch. A horse will run like the dickens in the wind and pay no mind to where it's running to, and you could be on it. A horse to draw his cart to town was a luxury he could not yet afford. He was still working with Millie. It was okay, too, because in a way, he had more than a lot of others. Not a lot, but enough for him and his family to survive. Growing up, Abigail and Matilda lived the typical *Little House on the Prairie* life. Her pa worked the fields and her momma did all the work inside the house. The two sisters had their routine as well, a typical load of chores for a small farm. That meant up at 5:00 A.M.

to fetch fresh water from the well to wash up and to cook with, collecting chicken eggs to make breakfast, milking Bessie, the family cow, feeding their four chickens, their one hog, Kirby, and Millie the mule. Didn't sound like much, but it was a lot. School wasn't far, only a little over a mile. The girls walked the road, as did most of the children. The school wasn't more than one room, with an outhouse behind it. Wooden logs made long benches and the children sat doing their lessons at long wooden picnic tables. When Abigail didn't have school, she would have to help her pa with plowing the field. Matilda was still too young to work the field. The family worked hard and barely made it by. Scraped and scrounged to get through the Great Depression of the 1930s. It wasn't easy, but the family survived through hard times. And just when things seemed to be getting a little better, they just got worse.

"What do you want me to do, Arhris. We ain't got no choice. Roosevelt has declared war. Pearl Harbor is gone, the Japs just blew it off the map. What do you want me to do? America is going to war. What if I get called to serve my country? I have to serve my country. Who's gonna help provide for the farm until I get home, you? Are you nuts? You're gonna need to hire a hand, you understand. If I sell Bessie, you'll have nothing. I'll be gone. I'm doing this for you and Matilda. Abigail is fourteen, come on. My daddy would have got her moved on."

"John, please, John, not Abigail, please. There has to be another way, John. She's too young, she's not old enough, she's not even got her period. We just can't."

"We can, Arhris, and we will, and that's that, dagnabbit. Just because she's slow with breeding don't mean nothing, she's ready. She's a grown woman, for Pete's sake, she's gonna end up pregnant, then what? You see them boys staring her down when we go to town. We don't got no choice. Winter's coming, Arhris, you're gonna need wood for fire. I can cut Kirby up to get you through the season, and there's the chickens, but you're gonna need Bessie, Arhris. Abigail is just another mouth to feed. Besides, Mr. Fothergill says he'll give us a pretty penny for her, a pretty penny, and he said he'll take good care of her. His money will help you run this farm and cover you while I'm gone, don't you understand? He's gonna make sure she gets to finish her schooling and what not. I made sure of that. And, she'll be close by, only a few towns from here, less than a hundred miles. I just don't see no other way, just don't."

"There has to be another way."

"Well, there ain't. There ain't no other way. Mr. Fothergill said he'd be here later this afternoon, so . . . be best if you go on now and get Abigail packed up."

"But . . ." said Arhris, pleading with her husband.

"Woman, I say the law," said John Wright, flexing his suspenders, ready to strike her down for being disobedient. "Now, she's going and that's that. Mr. Fothergill's fixin' to marry her and take care of her and you need to have her ready. You hear me, Arhris?"

"Yes, John, I can hear you, you're hollering at the top of your lungs. How can I not?" asked Arhris, in the tone of a child, then mumbled under her breath as she watched John turn his back to her and leave the room.

"Is that some kind of backtalkin' tongue-lashing you mumbling about?" he asked with his left eyebrow raised.

"No, I'm just humming, that's all . . . if it's all right wit' you," she said, cursing him silently under her breath.

"I reckon it's not, if I can't understand what you're saying," he commented before walking away. "Don't need to hear you or understand you no way. Don't even know why you speak at all. Just a waste of air if you ask me," he told himself as he closed the door behind him and walked down the hallway, continuing his personal conversation to himself.

It was the saddest day of Arhris's life to see her daughter sold away to some stranger, but she had no choice or say in the matter. What could she do? She was a woman, and unfortunately, in the 1940s a woman was nothing more than property and was just not allowed to disobey.

Abigail seemed to sense something wasn't right, walking up the dirt path from the main road. She saw a strange man standing next to her pa. He looked at her and her sister and smiled kindly.

"Who's that?" asked Matilda.

"I don't know, Tildie," said Abigail as she watched her father counting out what looked like a lot of money.

As they got closer to the house, Abigail saw two pieces of luggage on the porch. *I wonder where Pa is going?*

"Abigail, come on over here and let me talk to you. This here is Mr. Fothergill."

"Hello," said a young smiling Abigail.

"Hello," said a middle-aged, tall, medium-built man with a receding hairline, wearing pants, a clean white shirt and a matching suit jacket.

"Um, well, Abigail, this here is Mr. Fothergill and . . . um . . . well, he done come to take you on home with him. He's gonna marry you, you understand."

Abigail looked at her father standing tall and firm. He had the look of a cat who had just swallowed a canary.

"I don't understand, Pa."

"Well, um . . . Mr. Fothergill here, he's gonna take care of you and you're gonna go live with him."

"But, I don't want to live with him, I want to live here, with you and Momma and Tildie. Daddy, please, don't send me away. Please, I'll milk Bessie every day, Pa, and I'll do all my chores. And you don't have to do no plowing, I'll do every lick and I'll wash all the clothes for Momma, hang 'em on the line, nice and neat, and I'll cook, Pa. I can cook . . ." But the more she spoke, the more she knew she was wasting her breath. The more she spoke the more she knew she was already leaving. The more she stood there pleading with her father, the more she realized that the money he had been counting was the money Mr. Fothergill had paid for her. The more she spoke, the more Mr. Fothergill realized he was getting his money's worth. *Hell, she's barely a child, and she can cook, too.* She looked at Mr. Fothergill with pleading eyes full of tears.

"Don't mean no harm, mister, but please don't take me from my family."

"It's gonna be okay, I'm gonna take good care of her," said Mr. Fothergill as he took Abigail by her arm. She tried to pull away, but his grip was too firm.

"Ma, please, Ma, please don't let him take me. Pa, please . . ." she began to beg as Mr. Fothergill dragged her on over to his horse-drawn carriage.

"Momma, where's that man taking Abigail?" asked Tildie as her mother covered her mouth and ran inside the house crying. Tildie just stood to the side, watching a screaming Abigail being

led away by some stranger as her father stood alone, patting his
pocket, daydreaming about a horse, a rich, smooth, brown horse
with a white patch between his eyes. He had already seen her,
she was a mare, so she could birth. He'd pick her up tomorrow,
just in case the draft came through. Once Mr. Fothergill and
Abigail were out of sight he turned to Tildie. "All right now,
ain't no need standing out here all night long, might as well go
on inside. What's done is done, cain't go back, cain't go back,
Tildie."

It would be two years before Abigail saw her family again.
And the only reason she returned home then was that her father
had been killed in the war. Ray Fothergill made the trip back to
Murfreesboro so Abigail could pay her final respects.

"What you looking all confused for, Abigail, come on, let's
get going on now," ordered Ray in his usual casual tone. "Just
standing around going nowhere," he muttered.

"I want to see my pa laid to rest and all, it's just that, I don't
think the baby can take no carriage ride that long, that's all,"
said Abigail rolling her hands around her expanded belly.

"Aww . . . shucks, are you really serious?" He began to laugh
at her. "Dagnabbit, that's what's in that brain of yours," he said,
plucking at the side of her head. "Well, a few bumps here and
there sure ain't hurting you or no baby. Baby, baby, baby, Abigail, I sure will be happy when that thing gets here so I don't
have to hear about it no more."

Abigail stood quietly as she blocked Rayford Fothergill's
nerve-wracking babbling out of her head. She remembered the
day her daddy had sold her, sold her like a slave and didn't think
twice, didn't even blink. She remembered her mother's face, her
sorrowful eyes and her pain-filled smile. The dirt path led up to

the farmhouse from the main road and Abigail remembered the last time she saw it. She was being dragged away by the meanest man in the whole wide world. As soon as the horse-drawn carriage stopped moving Abigail could see Matilda. She was eleven years old, running up the hill to the front of the house so that she could greet her.

"Oh, my God, wait till Momma sees you. Wow, look at your belly. I almost didn't know who I was looking at." Tildie hugged her sister, and Abigail kissed her face a thousand times. Neither sister paid much attention to the funeral or the pastor; instead they sat in the pew talking as if they hadn't talked in a lifetime.

"I got to run away, and far, far away, where cain't nobody find me."

"Well, if cain't nobody find you, how will I?" asked Matilda.

"Well, I don't know. I guess I'll have to send you a postcard. One of them postcards with a big fancy city on it so you'll know where I am and that I'm okay."

"I sure do miss you, Abigail. Nothing's been the same since you been gone. Everything sort of changed, you know. Nothing's been the same."

"Really?"

"Yeah even Ma and Pa stopped speaking after you left."

"They did?"

"Yup, sure did."

Knowing that made Abigail feel all the better. She reached over and patted her mother on her back. She was so glad to be back in the company of her family that she didn't know what to do. She was even happier to be away from evil-ass Ray Fothergill. And the fact that her father was gone was a wonderful excuse to see Momma and Tildie again. It had been so long. The

only time she began to cry that day was when it was time to go
back home.

"Let's go, Abigail," said mean man Ray.

"Cain't I just visit with Momma and my sister just a little
longer?"

"No, come on, we best be getting on down the road before it
gets too dark out here," he ordered.

"I got to go," said Abigail, lowering her head and hugging her
sister.

"Don't cry, Abigail, don't cry," said Tildie as she let her sister
go. "Here, I picked these from our garden for you," said Tildie,
passing her sister a tiny bouquet of daisies.

"You know I love these; they're the happiest flower in the
world."

"Hey, we're gonna make a trip to see you once you have that
baby, you hear now?" added her momma, watching her two girls
say good-bye.

"Yeah, Momma, that would be nice. I just don't know if I can
wait to see you until then."

"Look at me," said her mother, taking her face and holding it
in her hands. "We'll be together again, and I'm always with you,
Abigail, always. You'll be fine, just stay strong. God has a plan
for you, Abigail, God has a plan."

Abigail, with the help of Rayford, pulled herself up into the
carriage.

"Goodness, Lord of mine, you are getting heavy, Abigail,"
said Rayford, catching his breath. "My leg almost buckled out,
and I swear I thought I was going to fall."

Wish you had fallen down, thought Abigail as she waved good-
bye. *God has a plan, just be strong.*

*   *   *

God had a plan all right, a plan for Abigail to run away in the middle of the night, and that's exactly what she did. When Rayford Fothergill got up looking for breakfast the next day, he found a note that had two words written on it: "good riddance." He never saw or heard from Abigail again.

She made her way through the dark, lonely, deserted night, moonlight shining through the pines and the tall oaks as she made her way to town. She hopped on the coal train with nothing but twenty-two dollars and fifteen cents. Back then, that was a small fortune, considering a gallon of gas was only twelve cents. She headed north, all the way to Philadelphia.

The year was 1944, and one month later, she gave birth to a baby girl, at Pennsylvania Hospital. The baby was stillborn. Doctors said the umbilical cord had choked the baby through the passageway. There was nothing they could do. The afterbirth remained, and they performed a surgery, which caused complications, and the outcome was that she would never be able to have children, ever again. Or at least that's what she was told by the doctors.

Once again, God always has his own plan, and twenty years later, she found herself, at thirty-six years old, sitting in a doctor's office in downtown Philadelphia, words ringing through her ears like sirens.

"You're pregnant!"

She was speechless, to say the least, and kept thinking of all the years that had passed by. She always thought the doctors had been right, as she hadn't used protection and had never conceived. It was a miracle, an act of God, truly it was. She was happy, so happy she began to cry. But her tears of joy quickly turned to tears of sorrow.

"What do you mean, pregnant?" The look on Gilbert Taylor's face said it all.

I should have never told him. Look at him, what is he thinking?

Gilbert Taylor didn't know what to say. He had a wife and a family. Yes, he cheated, but so did all his friends.

"You said you couldn't get pregnant."

"I can't, I mean, I did . . . it's like a miracle."

It wasn't a miracle for Gilbert and he didn't share her joy. The funland express had just reached its final destination. He wasn't sure how to handle her, but he knew he had to handle the situation with caution. She needed to understand that he couldn't leave his wife, and he couldn't be a father to her baby either. The best he could do was to help her financially. She had served a lot of years at his carpet warehouse.

"I just don't know what to say. I don't want a baby with you. It's just too complicated for me."

Abigail was devastated, and the thought of raising a baby without a husband in 1964 was even more devastating. If Gilbert Taylor didn't want to be a father to her baby, he didn't have to be, but he would have to pay. Gilbert would simply cut a check and live his life with his wife, living a lie, keeping Abigail and her baby a secret.

Deep down Abigail was tortured. She had always believed Gilbert would leave his wife for her and they would be together. A baby was nothing more than the perfect reason to act now. Instead, he shunned her, wanted her to disappear, and the next thing she knew Gilbert had laid her off, claiming lack of business. He still, however, paid her. The entire time she was pregnant, he just paid her to stay away. Abigail got through the nine months like a breeze. The pregnancy was easy and trouble-free.

The day her water broke she immediately called a cab to come take her to the hospital. She went in her bedroom, got the hospital bag she had prepacked and had waiting and ready to go, then called Gilbert. She dialed his number and listened as the phone rang.

"Hello," he said.

She heard his voice but remained silent. He said hello once again. It was the one chance she had to have him by her side. Instead of telling him her water had broken and she was in labor, she hung up the phone. A weight suddenly lifted, and a voice told her everything would be all right. And it was. The nurse handed Abigail a tiny baby wrapped in a bundle. She looked down at her newborn, eyes barely open. It was as if she were smiling. And for the first time in a long time, ever since the day her daddy sold her away, Abigail felt she had something to truly smile about. *Daisy, your name is gonna be Daisy.* And so it was, Daisy Mae Fothergill. Fothergill after Ray, the married name Abigail still carried, and Daisy because everything was happy now. She thought of her sister and her mother and the last time they were together. *God does have a plan for us, baby. Don't you worry, Momma's gonna take good care of you.*

"Please, Momma, please, tell me what to do. Please don't leave me. I can't make it out here without you. I can't, I don't have nobody that cares about me, I don't have nobody, Momma. Please god, give her back. Please give her back to me."

She finally called 911 and reported that her mother had passed away to the 911 operator. She answered a hundred questions, and of course, it would be hours before anyone came to remove the body. So Daisy prepared. She combed her mother's hair and dressed her up, put a little makeup on her, and gave her some perfume so she'd smell sweet.

"See, Momma, you look so pretty. So, pretty, Momma. I'm just going to miss you so much, I wish you was here right now. I wish you was here. I love you, Momma, I love you. I just don't know what I'm going to do without you. I just don't know."

Daisy sat quietly holding her mother's hand, as she waited for the paramedics to arrive. Her mother had left suddenly and without warning, leaving her feeling uncertain about life, uncertain about tomorrow, and scared to face it alone. Now with the passing of her mother, she realized she had no one in the world, no one who cared. A tear fell from her face and landed on her mother's palm. *"I miss you already,"* she said as she wiped the tear away.

The sky had turned from a burnt orange to a dark blue. Stars twinkled in the distance and hovered over the tattered city streets. The night air felt brisk, even though winter was months away. Saunta looked down at her son, who was clutching his book bag.

"How was school today?"

"Okay," he quickly responded.

"How was after care?"

"Okay," he again responded. Every day when his mother picked him up from after care, they would walk home together. She would ask him the same questions. Thank goodness, they only lived around the corner.

"I'm gonna make you some fried chicken wings and rice for dinner, you hear."

"Mmm, that sounds good. Mommy, can I go down the street to Malcolm's?"

"Yeah, for a minute, but take your book bag upstairs first and then you can go, okay?"

"Okay."

Saunta held the door for her son and followed him inside the apartment row home on the 2500 block of Somerset Street. They walked through the vestibule and up the flight of stairs. Just as Saunta reached in her purse and began to feel for her keys, a dark man, wearing dark clothing and a dark ski mask and dark gloves, jumped her from behind.

"Oh, my god, *heellpp*!" Saunta screamed as the dark figure pulled a gun and shot her in the chest.

"Mommy, no. Don't hurt my mommy." The young fellow charged the dark figure after seeing his mother gunned down and ran into him, almost knocking him down. He kicked and punched the dark figure, unafraid of the chrome barrel pointed at his head.

"POW!"

Another gunshot rang out as the little boy fell backward and lay silently still next to his mother.

The assailant grabbed Saunta's purse and ran back down the stairs, through the vestibule, and out the front door. After he was safely away from the crime scene, he pulled off his ski mask and put it in his pocket. He rummaged through the purse, pulling out Saunta's wallet. He took her ID and her keys and threw the purse in the trash.

"What's going on, Nard?"

He heard a voice call out to him as he turned around.

"Yo, what's happening, man, been a long time, my brother," he said, extending his hand.

"Sure has, how's it going?"

"I'm good, I'm good," said Nard as he shook an old acquaintance's hand.

"Take it easy, brother."

"Yeah, you too, man, take it easy," said Nard as he walked down the block, hopped in his car, and kept it moving.

UP SIDE IS DOWN

Hey, Ross, ballistics in on the Three Musketeers, yet?"

"Sure are. I got everything right here on my desk. Here you go, big guy," she said, tossing the folder to Delgado.

"You were right, you were god damned right."

"What?" questioned Ross, dying to know what she was right about again.

"You said there was another guy and you're right. The bullets that they took out of this guy, Jeremy Tyler, and Lance Robertson don't match the weapons at the crime scene. I should have known."

"What about the other guy?" asked Merva.

"The bullet in him matched one of the guns at the scene, but the bullets in the other two guys got a zero match."

"So, we got a killer on the loose?"

"Pretty much."

"Captain Dan isn't going to be happy; not a killer on the loose. Even worse, Mayor Goode is going to have his ass in a sling if we don't get this guy off the streets, like say in forty-eight hours."

"Yeah, yeah, Ross, I know. I know," said Delgado, realizing that he was just about to have his plate piled real high with tons of shit. Shit that he personally didn't want to have to eat. *Why do I always get the crappy cases? Dammit!*

"Listen, we got to get back out there and if we got to, hit every house and every apartment, until we find someone that knows something."

"Honing and his partner are covering the witnesses. I spoke to him earlier, he said no one is talking, no one knows anything. He told the captain in his report that a young kid who lived down the hall seemed to want to say something, but his mother refused, pulled him back in the apartment and shut the door in his face, saying they didn't know nothing. I think the captain said to bring the kid in for questioning."

"Did he?"

"Yeah, they're gonna bring him in."

Just then the phone rang. Detective Ross answered.

"What? You got to be kidding me."

She hung up the phone. "Come on, we got another homicide," she said to Detective Delgado, who was still reading the forensic findings folder.

"Where at?"

"That's the thing, you'll never believe it," she said looking at him as if an idiot could figure it out.

"The 2500 block of Somerset Street?"

"Bingo, come on, let's go."

*　　*　　*

The next morning the coroner from the medical examiner's office finally showed up to remove Daisy's mother's body from the apartment at around five-thirty. It appeared she had suffered a stroke. The coroner's office sat Daisy down and asked her many questions, filled out some forms, had her sign some papers, and then carried Abigail Fothergill away in a black body bag. The coroner said they were taking her to Temple Hospital where they would perform an autopsy on the body. Once the autopsy was complete, the body would be released to the funeral home of her choice.

After the coroner was gone Daisy picked up the phone. She had a short list of people that she knew she would have to notify. The first on her list was Aunt Tildie. Matilda Wright had married three times, but she only had one child, by her last husband, a daughter named Kimmie Sue. It was the strangest thing, but each and every one of her husbands had died from a heart attack, leaving her a widow. After the first husband, Tildie got smart and made sure she had insurance on the others. She made out like a fat little rat. Natural disasters, death, loss, whatever could hurt you financially, you could for the most part be protected against by insurance. Daisy let the phone ring several times before Tildie answered.

"Auntie Matilda, it's me, Daisy, I have some bad news . . ."

"Oh, no," said Tildie before she began to cry. "Let me call you back." It would be some time before Tildie got it together. Her sister Abigail had been the only family she had left, besides her daughter, Kimmie, and the truth was, Tildie had been planning to visit Abigail this summer. It had been so long since she had last seen her sister, sixteen years to be exact.

When Abigail was younger and more able to get around, they

spent the summers together in Murfreesboro where they had grown up. Every year around springtime, Abigail would make her way back down South where she had come from. And each and every time she made her journey and got safely back home to Philadelphia, the South would just keep calling her back. Something about walking in the footprints of lost time just brought back the most bittersweet memories. Her ma and her pa, her fox terriers, the farmhouse they lived in, the farm they had, the chickens, the horses, the pigs, the cows, the goats, the mule, and the rows and rows of corn her daddy minded were like a never-ending picture in a never-ending picture frame that flashed her mind in and out of places she had been in her lifetime. All the memories of her childhood she could always find in her travels back to Murfreesboro.

For the past year and a half, Matilda had been saving pieces of her Social Security check. Her plan was to fly out of Nashville nonstop to Philadelphia, spend a week with her sister, and then go back down South. Now, it was too late. Her older sister was gone. It was a feeling of loneliness that Matilda had never felt in her life. It was one thing to lose her ma and pa. That made her no one's child. It was another to lose her last and only family member. Seemed like all her memories of her and her sister growing up on the farm flashed in front of her, and she broke down in a pool of tears, feeling lonelier than she ever had in her life. She wanted to see Abigail, had to see her, had to bid her one last good-bye, and in her heart she knew the journey to Philadelphia from Murfreesboro would be well worth it. She explained the situation to her daughter, Kimmie, whom everyone nick-named Kimmie Sue, and they began their trip to Philadelphia for Abigail's funeral.

"I'll call you from the road and let you know we're all right."
Tildie called Daisy back and let her know that her family, what
little she had, was on the way and everything would be all right.
Daisy hung the phone up feeling a tad bit relieved. She knew
her aunt would be there for her. She had also felt better knowing
that she'd have someone there to lean on. She had never thought
in a million years that her mother would pass so unexpectedly.
Daisy drew in a deep breath as she wiped the tears off her face.
She had to make another call, to Hawkins Funeral Home on
Fifty-fourth and Haverford. She spoke calmly with one of the
directors and began making arrangements for her mother. Daisy
had it all figured out, and she ordered nothing short of the finest
for her mother to be laid to rest. She agreed to meet the director
at the hospital once the body was released by the medical examiner. As long as there was no foul play, the results of the autopsy
would be in shortly and the death certificate would be issued.
And that was all she needed, that death certificate.

Her next phone call was to the insurance company that
had issued a life insurance policy on her mother. She pressed
the number to speak with a representative. Daisy was nervous
and overwhelmed looking at the policy paperwork. *One hundred thousand dollars, damn, that's a lot of money right there.* She
couldn't help it, thoughts of cussing Calvin's evil ass out ran
through her mind.

"Get on out of here," she could hear him shouting now.

*"Fuck you, Calvin. I don't need you or this sorry dump you fake
ass pimp."*

"Hello, ma'am, are you there?" the representative asked a second time.

"Oh, I'm sorry, yeah, I'm right here," Daisy said as she stopped daydreaming.

She gave the woman all the pertinent information as she read it off the policy declaration page she had found in her mother's bedroom. She gave the operator the policy number and waited while she was placed on hold.

After a few seconds the representative came back to the line.

"I'm sorry, ma'am. It appears that policy was canceled for non-payment five months ago. Do you have another policy number you'd like me to search for you?"

"What?" Daisy asked, not hearing her clearly. "What do you mean, canceled?"

"Well, ma'am, the policy was canceled for nonpayment. We sent out a notice to your mom and it doesn't look like she re-sponded to it. And the policy won't stay open if it's not paid up. I'm so sorry."

"No, wait a minute, I got the paperwork right here, it's for one hundred thousand dollars."

"Yes, ma'am, but back in May we didn't receive a payment, and in June a cancellation notice was sent out, and after we didn't receive the payment in June the policy was canceled. I can check another policy for you, if you like."

Why didn't she tell me? There's no life insurance? How am I going to bury her?

"Ma'am, I'm sorry, would you like me to check another policy for you?"

No, bitch, check the policy I got right here. Fuck, how will I bury my momma?

"Umm, no, ma'am, that won't be necessary, thank you."

"I'm sorry I couldn't be of better service to you. Have a wonderful day."

"Eat a happy dick!" Daisy wanted to scream so bad, but she didn't.

"You, too, thank you."

Just as she hung up the phone the funeral director rang.

"Hello," Daisy answered.

"Ms. Fothergill, I got that quote for your mother's services for you. It's only $8,762.23," the director said, quite charmingly.

Eight thousand dollars, is he crazy? She's dead, not alive, I'm not spending no eight thousand on no dead person.

Daisy couldn't think straight. It was simply overwhelming. Her mother's passing over, no insurance policy, no hundred thousand dollars, and a funeral director trying to G her out of eight grand. *Lord have mercy.*

"I'm so sorry, sir. I just got off the phone with the insurance company. It turns out Momma doesn't have no life insurance to cover this. I just don't know what I'm gonna do."

There was a pause for a moment, and by the time the director was finished feeling Daisy out, realizing she was broke and had no money to bury her dead mother and no policy to sign over to his funeral home, there was only one possibility left.

"Well, we can pick her up from the coroner's, cremate her, and place her ashes in a lovely small urn for you for only $1,987.92."

That's my two thousand from my investigator, Daisy thought to herself, her plans now really ruined.

"Ma'am, would you like to do that?" he asked her again.

Having no other options, she agreed.

"Fine, then, I'll meet you at the hospital when the body is ready and you can sign the release there."

She hung up the phone, lay down on her mother's bed, and wiped the tears from her eyes. Daisy was tired and wished she could take a midmorning nap. But she only had a few hours before she would have to meet the director at the hospital. She picked herself up, grabbed her pocketbook, and locked the apartment door behind her. She saw the mailman as she made her way downstairs.

"Hello, I'm 3C," she said, extending her hand so he wouldn't put the mail in the box. "Thanks," she said as she fanned through the envelopes. *Ooh, Momma's Social Security check.* She knew that envelope. It was either Social Security or a tax refund, but the brown-windowed envelope with the Statue of Liberty chick always meant some dough. She opened the envelope: *Eight hundred, fifty-nine dollars and thirty-two cents. Dag, Momma, I need this money,* she said to herself, knowing that technically it wasn't right to cash her dead mother's Social Security check, but what the hell. She was a signer on the bank account, so technically it couldn't be that bad.

Detective Delgado and Detective Ross walked into the ICU ward and over to the nurses' station. They asked for Saunta Davis and were pointed over to bed thirteen.

"Ma'am, I'm Detective Delgado and this is Detective Ross. We are here to help find the person who did this. May we ask you a few questions?"

"She's really heavily sedated," a nurse said. "So, if she doesn't respond, you might want to come back, just keep that in mind."

"Thank you, we will," said Ross, smiling at the woman, wanting desperately to let her know they did not need her advice at all.

"Ms. Davis, do you remember what happened?" Delgado asked.

Saunta barely opened her eyes, her mouth dry and her body feeling not much pain, thanks to her morphine drip. She had just come out of recovery, after being operated on for the better part of the night.

"DaShawn," she whispered, in such a low voice Delgado couldn't make out what she was saying.

"Ms. Davis, do you know who did this to you?" Ross asked again, realizing the woman could speak.

Saunta, her eyes barely open, looked at Detective Ross and shook her head "Yes," then nodded back to sleep. Detective Delgado was ready to shake her back awake.

"Excuse me, I'm Dr. Sternberger, and this is my patient."

"Yes, I'm Detective Delgado, and this is my partner, Detective Ross. We're here investigating the shooting of Ms. Davis and the murder of her son," Detective Delgado said, extending his hand to the doctor.

"I understand that, but she can't answer your questions right now. She's heavily sedated and needs rest. As soon as she comes out of sedation, I will call you, but you will have to wait until I feel she is up to answering your questions."

Ross immediately looked at her partner, knowing what could possibly come out his mouth next, and quickly stepped in. "Thank you so much, Dr. Sternberger. You know, it's so important for us to bring her assailant to justice, we just need you to contact us the minute you feel she's ready to answer just a few simple questions."

"You have my word, I will."

"Thank you," said Delgado, being polite, as they all shook hands.

The two detectives made their way out of ICU as Merva shook her head at her partner. "Don't you know you won't get no bees with vinegar."

"I'm not interested in bees, I'm interested in finding a killer that's running around the streets of Philadelphia on the loose."

"Well, you sure won't find him like that."

Just as they were exiting the elevators, a young woman wearing blue jeans, a light blue T-shirt, sneakers, and a gray sweater bumped into them as she brushed between them trying to catch the elevator.

"Oops, 'scuse me," she said as the elevator doors closed.

"Wow, did you see her eyes?" said Delgado. "They were an odd green."

"I didn't know you like black girls," joked Ross.

"Why do you think I keep you around?"

"Oh, I thought it was for my charming personality and stunning good looks."

"Stunning good looks and charming personality?" he jokingly questioned.

"Whatever, I'm hungry."

"That's not surprising."

"Yeah, I got a taste for a Lee's Hoagie House."

"Let's go eat, wait and see if Dr. Sternberger will let us talk to this Davis woman any time soon. I have a gut instinct she knows who shot her and she knows something about the Three Musketeers from down the hallway."

"My gut's telling me tuna, mayo, provolone, sweet peppers, lettuce, tomato, salt, pepper, and oregano."

"I'm serious, Ross."

"So am I."

Calvin watched the floor and the bar. He took notes of every little thing, who was at what table, who was dancing, who was on a lap, who was going in the back, who was drinking and how much. He counted every last drop of liquor in his bottles and watched the bartenders like a hawk. They had better not even think of stealing one penny from him. No, Mr. Stringer was on his job. At the end of the day, everybody around there knew who was in charge.

"What's the matter with Daisy? She don't seem like herself," he asked Dallas as he sat at the bar and watched all the transactions around him.

"Yeah, I think her momma died. Trixie was saying something about Daisy. She's trying to hold it together," said Dallas as he wiped off the bar with a clean rag. "You want another one?" he said as he looked at Calvin holding up his shot of Royal Crown.

"Naw, naw, I'm good," said Calvin after slinging the shot back. He got up and walked over to where Daisy was hanging upside down from a pole on the left-hand side of the stage.

"Come on down here and let me talk to you," said Calvin, yelling above the bass, looking up at Daisy.

"What, can't you talk to me right here?" she hollered down to him.

"Your titties is hanging upside down," he hollered back.

"What?"

"Your titties," he said pointing.

"What about them?" asked Daisy as she tried looking upward at them dangling downward toward her chin.

"They're upside down," he hollered.

"What's that got to do with your mouth?" she asked him back as he began to grow irate.

"Look, get down here so I can talk to you," he said, watching her turn her body upright and slide down the pole.

"What, Calvin, can you talk to me now because my titties ain't upside down no more?"

"Don't be sassy," he barked, pointing a finger at her. "Come on, let's go in my office. I want to talk to you."

"Aww, Calvin, come on, you just looked me over yesterday," said Daisy, figuring he just wanted to get his rocks hard feeling on her as usual. He could try it all he wanted, she saw the bulge from the crotch in his pants every time he pretended to be some type of Mad Hatter gyn inspecting the goodies between her legs.

"Daisy, come on in here and sit down."

Daisy went in his office, removed her thong, and sat down in the chair next to his desk.

She knew, like everybody else, that you weren't allowed to wear clothes in Calvin's office. Whenever you were in the office, that meant business, and Calvin's line of business was pussy, and while in his office, that's what he wanted to see.

"What's going on with you?"

"What you mean, Calvin? Nothing."

"Man, I'm watching you out there and I don't know what you're doing. You look . . . awkward, off balance, no rhythm, no sex appeal, just a body hanging upside down. What's going on?"

"Calvin, I'm sorry. I just got so much going on. My momma died and I just been—"

"Your momma died?"

"Yeah, four days ago. She was all I had," said Daisy, fighting back tears. "And I ain't have no money, so I can't bury her, and my aunt is coming, but she don't know I had Momma cremated."

"Wasn't no insurance to bury her?"

"Nope, the policy lapsed for nonpayment."

"Well, don't start getting sad on me. Pull yourself together, Daisy. It's going to be okay. I'm sorry to hear about your momma. I think it probably be best if I let you take some time. Sometimes, in cases of death, in this line of business, the two don't mix."

"I can't take off Calvin, I need the money. I need my tips. I have to work," she said. She appreciated the gesture, but realistically it just wasn't economical.

"Don't worry about the money. Here, take a hundred dollars from me. It's something I want you to do for me."

Daisy looked at the money as if Calvin were insane. *What the hell am I gonna do with a measly hundred dollars?*

"Listen, I've been thinking. And with your mother passing and all, this might be just what you need right now anyway. Yeah, this could work out better for you and for me," he said, throwing out brighter possibilities her way.

"What, what you talking about, Calvin?"

"I think it might be better if I put you over in my new spot. What do you think?"

"The Honey Pot?" she asked, confused.

"Yeah, I need you over there. I really do. You got a good cli-ent base from here and they'll follow you. Trust me, you'll make good money, more money than you make here, because you'll get to keep your extra tips all to yourself."

"For real?" said Daisy, thinking of Calvin's greedy fingers let-ting her touch her money. "Okay, I'm in, I'll do it, but Calvin, I need more than a hundred dollars to get me through the rest of the week."

"Aaww, damn, no you don't. See, there you go, always got to mess up a good thing," he said as he slid another hundred off the wad of cash he had in his pocket.

"Thanks, Calvin," said Daisy as she kissed his cheek. "You know what, Calvin. You sort of all right."

"You just sort of be all right when you come back to work. Shit, don't make no sense. All upside down on a pole, looking like you the one that died," he said, mumbling to himself.

Tildie and Kimmie Sue arrived two days later, just in time for the memorial service that Daisy had planned in her mother's honor. Tildie, a devout follower of the Trinity Spirit Worship House of God, was utterly dismayed by the fact that Abigail had been cremated. She literally refused to sit in the same room with the ashes and was so angry at Daisy once she found out what Daisy had done with her sister's remains that she cried her heart out.

"Why did you do that to my sister!" she screamed at Daisy. "Why didn't you call me? I would have buried her, I would have buried my sister. Why did you do that? Why?" Daisy didn't un-derstand faith or beliefs and the principles associated therewith, but she learned enough that day to know that the last thing her aunt would have done was cremate her mother.

After the memorial service, the three went out to eat. A small local restaurant that served soul food was only a few blocks down the street. Kimmie Sue was taken in by the big-city streets and big-city signs. The lights, the colors, the fast-moving traffic, and a brick on top of brick city opened Kimmie Sue's eyes to a world that she hadn't known existed. Her mother would be packing up and leaving to head back to Tennessee in the morning, and of course, Kimmie Sue would be going with her. She wished she didn't have to. She wished she could stay and get to know her cousin, get to know Philadelphia. It seemed like a nice town, with much to offer.

The next morning, Kimmie Sue and Aunt Tildie piled back into their Chrysler and made their way onto I-95 headed back to Tennessee. Daisy watched the car as it traveled down the block.

In her head, she could see her cousin. "I sure do wish I could stay right here with you. You are so lucky living in this big city and all. It's sort of scary. You don't get scared?"

"No, not scared, more tired than anything, I guess. City life is a harder life, I think, than living in the country. Just something about the concrete that makes living in the city a little tougher, I guess."

"I guess too," said Kimmie Sue. "But, I'm fittin' to come back here real soon."

"I want to come and visit you too, Cousin Kimmie Sue."

"Well, you're welcome, just come on down and I'll be waiting for you."

They hugged each other and then Kimmie Sue pulled out a small button from her jacket pocket.

"This was Aunt Abbie's." She handed the button to Daisy, who stood looking quite confused. "It come off her shirt one day. Momma said they were schoolgirls and it was the most embarrassing thing 'cause Momma said Aunt Abbie's titties flew out her shirt right smack in front of Wilson Carter, who everybody in the school had a crush on. Momma said Aunt Abbie wouldn't come out the house for a week, she was so embarrassed. Momma gave it to me and after she told me the story she said to always remember to keep my buttons buttoned so I don't reveal nothing that nobody needs to see."

Daisy looked down at the button and closed her hand. She squeezed her hand tight before letting the button slip through her fingers into the jacket pocket of her pea coat. She could hear her mother now, telling her she needed to button everything on her body. *Oh, Momma.*

"It's a good luck button too. I tell you ever since I started carrying that thing, I just felt so safe and secure. I figured since you're up here in this big city all alone now, you might need it to keep you safe too."

Kimmie Sue smiled and hugged her cousin before piling into the Chrysler. Daisy waved them off and turned back up the street to the door to the apartment. It felt odd and strangely lonely inside the apartment she used to share with her mother. She had never imagined life without her mother; she never had a reason to. But, now that she was all alone, she knew that life without Abigail would be different. Up until this point, she had a mommy and was someone's child. Now, those things had been stripped away, and she was simply Daisy Mae. She looked down at her watch.

I better get going, she thought to herself. Knowing Calvin with his constant five, five, five, she didn't want to be late for her first day at the Honey Pot.

GOTCHA

Please, excuse me, my patient really needs her rest. I thought I was being polite when I told you that once she is up to visitors and police interrogation, I would gladly call you," said Dr. Sternberger, feeling offended by their disdain for hospital policy. He was so riled, he began reaching for the phone to call security. The detectives in front of him would be removed from ICU.

"I'm sorry, Doctor, I just don't think you understand the urgency. We really need for her to ID her assailant from some of these photos. Really, this is critical, because he's still out there," said Detective Delgado, trying to remain calm, not curse, throw a tantrum, or, worst case, hurt Dr. Sternberger.

"Really, Doctor, we just need the opportunity to try. If she can't then she can't, but at least, for her sake and her little boy's sake, let us try," implored Merva, looking into the doctor's eyes, not understanding him at all. "If someone shot you and your son, wouldn't you want to ID him . . . if nothing else?"

"She is our missing link for us to get a killer off the streets and behind bars," added Detective Delgado.

The two of them spoke calmly to the doctor, with a hint of urgency. And of course it worked. The doctor gave them five minutes alone with his patient. She was still under the watchful eyes of ICU attendants. She had tubes sticking out from her body and connected to machines keeping all her vitals and stats for the doctors as they did their rounds. Detective Ross took her time talking and speaking to Saunta. Slowly Saunta opened her eyes. She never said one word. She didn't have to. The look of fear that covered her face as Detective Ross flashed Bernard Guess's head shot in her direction caused her to open her eyes as wide as they could go. She pressed back on the pillow and tears formed in her eyes. She looked scared at seeing the man's face.

"That's him," she whispered with a faint breath, reliving the feeling of being gunned down, the bullet entering her chest, piercing her rib, and lodging inside her. Leaving her in the Intensive Care Unit. She went into distress. Her blood pressure went up and a machine next to her bed started beeping. Dr. Sternberger came rushing into the room.

"She's losing pressure. Her heart rate is dropping. We're losing her!"

Tommy Delgado and Merva Ross stood over to the side looking like Lenny and Squiggy from *Laverne and Shirley* as they watched the doctors and nurses trying to stabilize their patient.

"Doctor, she's flatlined," said a blond nurse as Merva and Tommy heard a solid, steady tone, instead of the beeps that had been the echo of the ICU room.

"Oh, damn, she's dead?" questioned Merva as she leaned in and whispered into Tommy's ear.

"Yeah, I think we should get out of here before Dr. Stern-berger comes back over here and chews off our asses for fucking with his patient."

"Damn, he did say let her rest."

"Well, she will now," said Delgado, looking as if he was in fact the bird that swallowed the canary.

"Jeez, you are the worst."

"Yeah, come on, this looks bad. This isn't good. Let's get out of here," said Delgado, grabbing his partner's arm.

"At least we got our man, Bernard Guess," said Ross, looking at the brighter side.

"Yup, we got what we came for."

Once she got settled in at the Honey Pot, Daisy realized she had made the biggest mistake in her life. The Honey Pot was set up like an apartment. When you first walked in, there was a vestibule where the gentlemen would wait, seated patiently, unless they had an appointment scheduled. There was a receptionist, some tiny Asian girl who looked no more than fourteen, but was actually nineteen years old. She would take each man who came in for services into a seating area where they could wait to view the girls one by one. After viewing the girls they could pick who they wanted to give them a massage, if they had a preference. And once they had made their choice, they would disappear into one of the massage rooms just like magic.

Daisy needed her tips, and when the doorbell rang she was always ready, wearing a see-through negligee. She did her sexual seduction thirty-second lap dance for the gentlemen callers, letting them feel free to feel her up, or if she didn't do that, she'd take off her negligee and lie on the floor, sprawling herself wide open and making snow angels, but without the snow. Those were her secrets, and she was constantly picked.

Once inside the room, she would undress them and lie them on the table. Then she would stand at their head and massage them, always keeping her pussy in their view. As she rubbed them, they rubbed her, and when it was time to roll them over onto their backs, they would be rock hard, ready to drive their swollen muscles into her moist pussy. The only problem was that all her regulars, and the newcomers, were lining up, and as the weeks went by, Daisy found herself a sex slave inside the massage parlor. They weren't coming in asking for Daisy to just massage them, they expected the massage and a good quick fuck, all within thirty minutes. It was like their afternoon lunch break or a quick to-do task before going home at the end of the day. And they were lining up not just for Daisy, but for all the girls. Pretty soon, Calvin had to stop spending so much time at the Honey Dipper, because too much money was being made at the Honey Pot, and Daisy was his headliner, fucking and sucking more men in the course of a day than Vanessa Del Rio ever could in her life. It got to the point that liquor and e-pills simply numbed her from it all. And she simply did what she had to.

One night, while she was standing at the bus stop, her pager went off. It was Sticks.

He sure do got some nerve, where the hell has he been the last couple of months. Daisy couldn't help but to think of everything she had had to go through since Sticks had paid her that two grand. She had tried calling him, but he never answered her call or called her back. She had really needed him when her mother died. She just knew he'd help bury her mother. But he was missing in action and it had been two months since then. She went over to the pay phone and dialed his number back.

"Hey, Daisy, where you at? I'm over here at the Honey Dipper, but they said you don't work here no more."

"I don't, I work over at the Honey Pot now. Calvin moved me. Why?"

"'Cause my mans and 'em is having a bachelor party and I need you."

"I know you don't need me. Shoot, you don't even bother to call to see if I'm dead or alive," said Daisy, ready to hang up the phone.

"Dais, it ain't like that. I just been busy. Look, I got like two thousand dollars for you and another girl, that's a thousand apiece," said Sticks, trying to sound convincing.

Daisy heard him say two thousand dollars and her ears shot straight up off the side of her head. "How many girls you say you want?"

"Just two of y'all."

Daisy's brain started to overpower the e-pills from earlier and she put on her thinking cap. A new girl named Trixie who was working at the Honey Pot with her. *Maybe she'd like to come and make a couple hundred.* Daisy couldn't help but think to herself that she would be walking away with that two, or at least as close to that two as possible. Sure enough, Trixie was more than down; for $350 in her pocket, she was ready to do whatever Daisy needed her to. Unfortunately, Trixie had no idea that she and Daisy were walking into a trap when they walked through the door of the hotel room. Trixie and Daisy were repeatedly raped and sodomized by the bachelor party attendees. Both girls had been given champagne when they first got there. Gobbling it down and holding out her glass for more, Daisy never realized that she was being drugged. She was lucky she woke up at all after being slipped a mickey. When she woke up the next morning, she looked around the empty hotel room. Trixie was lying on the other full-size mattress that was side by side to hers. She looked at the clock: 10:38 A.M. Daisy had one hundred and one things to do before getting to the Honey Pot. She tried to stand, and her head began to spin. She sat back down. She reached over to the table and grabbed a Polaroid picture that was upside down.

Ohmigod, she whispered to herself as she looked at the photo of her body squished between two men. There was another photo of her giving head while having sex with someone else doggie style and Trixie doing the same, and then Trixie and Daisy doing men together, each other, etcetera, etcetera, etcetera. She looked around the room for her pocketbook. Quickly she fumbled through the purse. *The money, where's the money?* She thought carefully back to the night before. *Sticks paid me, right?* He had paid her before they started drinking. *But what the fuck was that he had me drinking? He drugged me, that he did for sure, and he done took back that money he gave me.* Quickly she finished putting her clothes on and grabbed her pocketbook. She looked at Trixie. *Should I wake her or let her sleep?* Daisy decided to leave her asleep. She walked out of the hotel room and made her way down the hall to the elevator. She had collected all the Polaroid pictures left around the room and quickly flicked through them as tears began to drop down her face. She couldn't believe that Sticks would rape her like that. Pass her around like she wasn't nothing and drug her up so she couldn't resist. *Shit, I know that damn Trixie is going to want the $350 I promised her.*

What the fuck am I going to tell her? She's gonna be mad. Daisy didn't even want to think about that argument. She would just have to deal with her later. Fortunately for Daisy, though she didn't know it at the time, the mickey they had slipped Trixie had left her in a real bad way.

Several hours later, housekeeping found Trixie walking the hallways naked and unable to identify herself. She seemed to be humming a nursery rhyme and had no idea who she was, where she was, the day of the week, the month, or what year it was. The hotel manager called 911 and an ambulance came for her and took her away. By the time Daisy got to the Honey Pot, the news of Trixie was all the girls were talking about.

"She was in some hotel and was drugged up, raped, and sodomized."

"I heard they say she's never going to come back right, like she's all messed up in the head."

"That mickey shit can fuck you up. I know this one girl, she real retarded now 'cause of that shit, and she was raped too. I wonder who did that to her?" said another girl, turning to see Daisy walk into the room. "Oh, hi, Daisy. Did you hear what happened to Trixie?"

"Yeah," said Daisy, "I heard. It's just unbelievable." Daisy didn't want the other girls to know she had taken Trixie to the hotel for Sticks's little get-together. She didn't want anyone to know she had anything to do with Trixie's condition at all. Rape and sodomy were criminal activity, and Daisy wanted nothing to do with a criminal investigation. *Damn, did anybody see us leave together last night? Shit, I hope not. What if Trixie phoned a friend and told them she was with me? Damn, damn, damn, I'll be suspect number one before the night is out.* With that cloud of gray news hanging over her head, Daisy just couldn't seem to get right. All night, she was off her marker. Truth was, she just didn't feel like working. It was too much, the night before, Sticks beatin' her for her two thousand dollars and then Trixie being drugged lay a little too heavy on her mind.

Quitting time couldn't come fast enough. Daisy was the first one out the door. Walking down the street to the bus stop, Daisy was so lost in her own translation of last night's events she wasn't paying attention and bumped into a passerby.

Her pocketbook fell to the ground and some of the contents fell out. In particular, Sticks's photo gallery collection. *Damn,* she thought as she quickly bent to pick her purse off the ground.

"Oh, I'm sorry. Here, let me help," said a kind voice, as the passerby bent to pick up one of the Polaroids that was lying face down.

"That's okay," said Daisy as she slapped the Polaroid back down on the ground and picked up the photo herself. "I don't need any help. Thank you," she said, making eye contact with a fine-looking brother, wearing a business suit at that.

"I'm so sorry. I was looking at my cell phone and I wasn't paying any attention to where I was going. Can you forgive me?" he politely asked.

"It was nothing. Of course, I'm fine. Thank you," she said as she adjusted her pocketbook over her shoulder.

"I'm Reggie Carter," he said as he extended his hand to her.

"I'm Daisy, Daisy Fothergill," she answered as she took his hand in hers.

"You know, I was just getting ready to go over to this tiny coffee shop and get a bite to eat. Would you like to join me?" he asked, looking every bit a nerd, glasses and all.

"Umm, no, no thank you. I must be getting on my way. But the offer is very kind of you."

"Well, maybe if you don't want to grab some coffee or a bite to eat now, maybe another time?" he politely asked, very much hoping to be able to share her company.

"Ummm, why not," Daisy said after carefully thinking it over. He seemed nice, well groomed, even though he wasn't very stylish. He was attractive, tall, brown, and seemed to be well educated.

"So, what do you do for a living?" he asked.

Daisy didn't have a response. For the first time in her life she felt shame at her occupation. She looked down at the Polaroid sticking out of her pocketbook and pushed it back down into the side of the purse.

"Ummm, I'm a receptionist for a physical therapy center," she said, lying through her teeth, knowing damn right well she gave out naked massages and whatever else came her way all day and night long.

"Oh, wow, that's great. I'm a home line of credit specialist for a mortgage company. You wouldn't need a line of credit, would you?"

"I don't own a home."

"Ooops, can't help you!" He laughed with her.

"Well, here's my contact information," she said after writing down her telephone number.

"Thanks, maybe we'll get together for dinner one night this week?"

"Sure, that sounds nice, just give me a call," she said as she realized her bus was approaching the bus stop.

"Take care," he said as she hurried to the corner stop.

"You too," she hollered back.

He looked at her number. She seemed really nice, attractive, and the plus side was that she had a day job. He had been looking for a nice woman he could make some moves with for quite some time now. Little did he know, she was far from a housewife, but she definitely had some moves he'd be interested in. He decided he wouldn't waste time and would be wining and dining her before the week was out.

SWEET DREAMS

It was like a dream come true. Reggie Carter was a knight in shining armor and had been sent from the angels above to love Daisy, and you couldn't tell her otherwise. Every day he wanted to see her, every night he was by her side. He even changed his cell phone number, tired of other women calling.

"I don't need nobody calling me but you, baby." Sure enough, that's what he told her. She should have known something wasn't right then and there, but love is blind, and Reggie Carter had Daisy walking around like she was Helen Keller.

As far as she was concerned, he was turning out to be heaven sent, a real man's man who doted on her. If she wasn't feeling well, you best believe Reggie would show up with every over-the-counter medication sold to man. If she had a headache, he'd rub her head. If she said her feet hurt, he'd rub her toes. If she had to shit, he'd be right there with toilet tissue balled up in his hand. And needing something was out of the question.

"Baby, you won't need for nothing. You hear me, Daisy, you

won't need for nothing. Maybe want, but never need. I will take care of you."

Who was he and where did he come from? Daisy just couldn't believe it. It was just too good to be true. She questioned everything about him. Everything, even his previous relationships, wives, children, retirement plans, everything. He had a medical card in his wallet and told her that he was the co-owner of a shoe store, on Thirtieth and Sansom streets across from the train station. He even took her there one day and, believe it or not, his business was thriving. He said he had no previous marriages and had no children. *He is amazing, just simply amazing.* Daisy knew she was in love, she was happy, and she was being taken care of. *Thank you, God, I just love him, he's really perfect. Really, perfect.* She just couldn't believe it was happening and it was happening oh so fast. He was always doing something for her. Refused to let her take the train and even told her that he was going to get her a car, so she wouldn't have to walk. Whenever he was coming over, he always asked if she needed anything. And he took her to the grocery store and bought food for the apartment every week. One day, Reggie came in with flowers and candy and it wasn't even Valentine's.

"Aww, baby, is this for me?" said Daisy, her arms reaching out for a large bouquet.

"Naw, baby, don't touch that. Those right there is for my momma. Don't worry though, I got yours right over there," he said, pointing to a larger-than-large bouquet that was lying on the kitchen counter. "Come on, I want to take you home to meet my momma, baby."

"Meet your momma? Why you didn't tell me? My hair ain't done or nothing."

"Girl, you ain't got to worry about that hair. Let me see the real hair and I'll tell you if everything is all right."

He pulled her pants down and she let him peek inside her panties. "Girl, you looking all right to me, come on, let's go."

Daisy felt like a queen. She had never ever had a man say he was taking her home to meet his momma, never. Reggie was good to her, but it had only been three months since she met him. But it had been the most wonderful three months of her life. Reggie was even talking about getting married and having a big wedding and everything.

"I don't have any family. My momma died and I don't know my father. I do have a cousin, Kimmie Sue, and my auntie Tildie."

Daisy couldn't help but to try to figure out who would sit on her side of the church. She could see Calvin Stringer and the girls from the Honey Dipper and the Honey Pot. *Oh, damn, not Calvin.* And then the worst sight of all, her many, many johns, and seated in the front row, that good-for-nothing Felix. *Hell no, no way.*

"What's the matter?" asked Reggie, startling her. He was wondering why her face looked pale with thought.

"Oh, god," she jumped, "you scared me to death."

"So, just Cousin Kimmie Sue and your auntie Tildie, huh?"

"Yeah, that's it."

"Well, I got some family, so we'll pack the church in."

He said he wanted children and told her how important children would be to their relationship. As far as Daisy was concerned, babies wasn't no problem. She was fertile Myrtle when it came to having babies. Even though she didn't have any, at twenty-one she had terminated six pregnancies, each and every one of them, and vowed that she wouldn't be careless ever again after the last.

The one problem that she did foresee was figuring out how to tell Reggie that she worked in a massage parlor and was fucking and sucking more dick on a daily basis than he could possibly imagine. Technically, she had him thinking that she was a receptionist for Zaslow, DeSimone, and Goldstein. It was pathetic. He'd drop her off at work, watch her walk into an office building, and figure she was at work all day. Little did he know, she'd wait in the lobby, then go catch the El line out to Kensington and be at the Honey Pot forty minutes later, getting dicked down all day long. She'd hop in the car when he'd come to pick her up, kiss him on the mouth, and act like it was nothing.

The only thing was, the more time she spent with Reggie, the harder and harder it lay on her conscience. She just couldn't stomach the sex acts. Every day, she'd pretend the strangers fucking her were Reggie and she'd come like a race horse, building her clientele. Then when she got home, Reggie would be on her and she'd pretend he was one of the strangers at the Honey Pot and come even harder, keeping Reggie feeling like he was the biggest winner. Reggie just loved being treated like a king. And if Daisy did nothing else, she made sure he knew he was king. She licked everything, including his asshole, and once he took her home to his momma, oh it was really on, that night when they got back to her apartment, he started telling her how much he loved her and how much he wanted to be with her. He even stressed to her how much his mother liked her.

"My momma told me I better marry you, girl. She said she wants you to give her some grandbabies. What you think, you think you could do that for my momma?" he said coyly.

"I sure can. Daddy, I can do whatever you want me to," she said as she sat on his lap and nibbled on his ear. That was all Reggie needed to hear. He knew he had her, mind and soul.

"What if I want to fuck you in your ass?"

That's it, Daisy thought to herself. She stood up, and began to slowly undress in front of him. She watched as the bulge inside his pants began to grow. She slipped out of her panties until she was standing in front of him completely naked. Then she got down on the floor, on her hands and knees doggie style. She turned around, looked behind her, and simply asked, "What you waiting for?"

Two weeks later Reggie dropped her off at the make-pretend office building. She went around the corner, caught the train to the Honey Pot, and sure enough, soon as she got inside Calvin was on her ass about being late.

"Look, dammit! Y'all always coming in this motherfucker late! Don't make me five your ass," hollered Calvin, holding his stupid hand up with his pokey fingers extended.

"I told you my boyfriend don't know and I got to catch the train and I don't mean to be late, Calvin, but if he find out . . . it'll just mess up everything."

"Mess up everything for who, you or me? Next time you late, I'm docking your ass five dollars every five minutes. Five!" he hollered at her again, still holding out his hand in her face.

"Someone's here to see you," said some Asian-looking chick Calvin had sitting naked at the front reception desk. *Where'd he find her?*

"See me? Who?"

"He's in room three, already paid for an hour massage. You better hurry."

Daisy opened the door to room three and peeked inside.

"I been missing you, Daisy Mae," said Felix as he licked his tongue at her. She immediately knew what that meant.

Yuck, how'd you find me? she thought to herself.

She knew she couldn't do this anymore. At least not while Reggie was in her life and if there was any chance she was going to have a man who loved her, and wanted to be with her, she couldn't jeopardize it anymore. She had been sneaking around long enough behind Reggie's back. She just couldn't do it anymore. She didn't want to. Besides, why should she risk losing a good man? Reggie said he wanted her to get pregnant, he said he wanted them to get married and even asked her would she like to help him find the new house he was planning on buying. He even gave her the number to a real estate agent and told her that their limit was five hundred thousand dollars. *Can you imagine me living in a five-hundred-thousand-dollar home?* Even she couldn't imagine it. Felix began to suck her chest, lick her nipples, and feel between her legs. The sex act itself was horrible, just too much to bear. Felix had this stale, cigarette breath and his fingers looked like he had been working on a chain gang, all dirty under the fingernails, and the thought of him touching her, licking her, and fucking her made her throw up, literally. She couldn't make it to the bathroom fast enough and left behind her a trail of vomit leading to the toilet where she buried her head.

"What the fuck!" Felix hollered. "God damn it, I didn't come here for nobody to throw up on me," said Felix as he wiped her vomit from his leg and foot.

"I'm sorry, I'm sorry," said Daisy as she crawled off the floor and ran out the door.

"Where the hell is you going?" yelled Felix down the hall.

All the commotion had the receptionist standing naked in the hallway. "Is everything all right, sir?"

"Hell no, ain't nothing all right. She's sick. Daisy done threw up in here all over the place. You done sold me some sick pussy and I want my money back!"

"Okay, sir, just one moment, I'll take care of everything, don't worry. Come back in your room and lie down, everything will be fine. I'll let Calvin know what happened right away. Don't worry," said the receptionist as she closed the door behind an aggravated Felix.

However, it wasn't fine. Calvin tried to straighten everything out, offered him another girl, but Felix didn't want her, he wanted Daisy.

"No, if I can't have Daisy Mae, then I want my money back," Felix ordered.

You best believe that Calvin was not a happy camper having to hand back the money that Felix had paid, but he had no choice.

"Daisy, get in here, now!" screamed Calvin.

Daisy walked through the door into the office of the Honey Pot and stared at Calvin.

"Calvin, look . . ."

"No, Daisy, you look. You in here is costing me money. If you so god damn sick, why didn't you stay home?"

"I didn't know I was sick. I just can't do it no more," she said as tears began to well up in her eyes.

"Do what?" asked Calvin, as if she was talking about something so horrific he needed time to figure it out.

"Do . . . this. I just can't, I can't."

"Can't?" questioned Calvin, his temper becoming irritated.

"No, I can't, I can't do this no more," said Daisy Mae, for once in her life standing up for herself.

"So you throw up on the man? No wonder he wanted his money back. You listen here, and you listen real good, I ain't got time for this shit, you hear me, Daisy Mae? You come up in here late all the god damn time, can't do your job 'cause you got a dead momma, and you know what, I say okay to that. But now you got some funky-ass nigga in your ear, feeding you a bunch of bullshit and now you can't do your job."

"This ain't no kind of job, Calvin. I swear this ain't."

"You insulting me, Daisy Mae, 'cause it sounds like you think you better than somebody."

"I'm better than this, Calvin. I'm better than this."

"No you're not, you no better than the rest of the girls," he said, ready to unleash his fury on her. "I don't know who you think you are, but when you ready to come on here and sell pussy for a living you let me know."

"I'm not for sale no more. I got a man who loves me and is going to take care of me. He said he wants to marry me."

"Bitch, is you crazy?" Calvin laughed at her so hard, he needed to grab the back of a single standing chair.

"Who the fuck are you laughing at?" asked Daisy, ready to attack Calvin and scratch out his eyeballs. How dare he laugh at her like that.

"You, Daisy, you're a real funny girl. You been stripping all your life, selling pussy all your life, and now all of a sudden you meet some man and you think he's going to marry you?"

"Yeah, he's gonna marry me."

"Yeah, you're killing me," said Calvin as he bent back up,

fixed his facial hair, and let go of the chair he was leaning on. "You can't make a ho a housewife, everybody knows that. Oh, but then he doesn't know you're nothing but a whore that's been fucked by the entire town," he said, throwing the money he owed her on the desk.

"Fuck you, Calvin, I quit," said Daisy, picking up the $213.

"Quit," he said, not really believing that she was serious. "Quit, you can't quit. You need me."

"You must be out your mind. I don't need this dump, and I damn sure don't need you!" said Daisy. She slammed Calvin's door behind her.

"Bitch must be crazy," Calvin muttered to himself as he opened the door and looked down the hall at a bunch of naked women eavesdropping. "What the hell y'all doing standing around? Get your asses back to work, dammit!"

"This is Monica Casey and I'm standing in front of City Hall. Here with me is Captain Daniel Fuentes of the Thirty-second Police Precinct. Captain Fuentes, there is a massive manhunt now taking place for the prime suspect in the Somerset murders."

"Yes, we are asking the public at this time to help capture the man identified as Bernard Guess of Twenty-third and Ridge Avenue, in North Philadelphia. Police believe he's extremely dangerous and armed. He's wanted in connection with the recent murders on the 2500 block of Somerset Street. Any information, tips, or knowledge of the murders or whereabouts of Bernard Guess can be phoned in to crime stoppers. The number is 1-800-55-CRIME. Again, that's 1-800-55-CRIME. There is a twenty-five-thousand-dollar reward for anyone who has any information that helps lead to the arrest of Bernard Guess."

"Okay, let's show the sketch of Bernard Guess for the public. Again, there is a twenty-five-thousand-dollar reward for any information leading to the arrest of Bernard Guess, the prime suspect in what police have begun to call the Somerset murders, where three people were murdered in a row home apartment building on Somerset Street on November 5 and two others, a woman and a nine-year-old boy, were murdered in the same row house one week later. The woman, identified as Saunta Davis, identified Guess before she died in Temple University Hospital. Police believe these murders are related. Police are also asking that until Guess is apprehended you use extreme caution and care."

Nard picked up the remote and turned the television off.

"Fuck," he whispered, then threw the remote down on the tattered mattress inside the studio apartment on Forty-third and Baltimore Avenue. *I got to get the fuck out of here. This tight-ass apartment. It's hot in this motherfucker and where the fuck did this broad go? Motherfucker asked this bitch to get some Chinese food. Shit don't take 101 minutes to get no Chinese food. What if she knows I'm wanted by the law? This bitch, what if she knows I'm on the run? I should've never let her go to the store. Fuck!*

Nard was so paranoid, he didn't know what to do. He did know that for twenty-five grand, he'd turn his own self in. The more he thought about it, the more he thought that was exactly what she was doing, and instead of her returning with Fong Wu's Chinese food, he was positive she would be returning with the police. He could see them now, banging down the door, weapons drawn, lasers flashing, and a barrage of metal bullets slamming him up against the wall. And if the police didn't somehow manage to Sean Bell his ass then he'd be arrested and his entire life would get flushed down the toilet.

He quickly gathered all evidence that he was ever in the apartment. *Maybe I'm bugging, maybe she's not turning me in.* He finished stuffing his few belongings into a dirty pillowcase and made his way up the fire escape and onto the roof. *We'll see if she comes back with Chinese food or the Thirty-second Precinct.*

Nard was pretty much stuck. Only a few more hours though and Sticks would have everything set up for him. The plan was to get him out of the city and down to Miami. Once he got to Miami, he'd take a private boat for a small fortune and sail out of the country to one of the seven hundred islands in the Bahamas. It didn't matter to him, as long as he wasn't arrested. He watched carefully as Cathy came around the corner carrying a bag of Chinese food. There was no sign of the police anywhere in sight.

"Wheeww," he said, letting out a sigh of relief. He grabbed the dirty pillowcase filled with his belongings and made his way back down to her apartment floor. She was standing at the door fumbling with the keys, trying to hold the food.

"What you doing in the hall?" she asked as he came around the corner.

"Nothing, man, getting ready to go outside and look for you. I'm so hungry, I can eat a horse. You was taking too long."

"I know, they was crowded and they didn't have nothing ready. So I had to wait."

Cathy Robbins was a small-framed, petite young girl, no more than twenty-one years old. She lived alone in her seven-hundred-square-foot studio apartment and worked as a salesgirl at the popular clothing store City Blue on Thirteenth and Market streets. She didn't have a steady boyfriend and she was smart enough not to have any children. Her mother had kicked her out when she was only fifteen and she never knew her father.

They went back inside the apartment and Cathy took the Chinese food into the kitchen. Nard flopped back down on the mattress, which was the only furniture in the unit besides an old chair that was in the corner next to an end table. She handed Nard a plate of shrimp fried rice and General Tso's chicken.

"I'm gonna take a shower, okay?"

"Yeah, sure. When I'm done, I'm gonna run downstairs."

"For what, where you going?" she asked, concerned.

"Nowhere. I'm just going to get a pack of cigarettes and take me a smoke."

"Oh, yeah, well do that down there. I can't stand no cigarette smoke. I don't know how people smoke them things," she muttered to herself as she closed the bathroom door.

Nard flicked on the television and watched as the picture came in full view. His face was large as day on the twenty-seven-inch Panasonic. He tried to flick the channel as quickly as he could, but dropped the remote.

"Police are looking for the suspect and crime stoppers has a twenty—"

He changed the channel before the reporter could finish her sentence.

"Don't say my name in this motherfucker. That's all I need, for this broad to figure some shit out."

Good thing Cathy didn't watch the news. He turned to Channel 17 and turned the volume up a bit. *No, fuck that, no television for her,* he thought to himself. He decided it would be best that while he went outside to call Sticks, she have no access to the outside world or the situation he had found himself in. He reached behind the entertainment cabinet and turned the TV off. Then he put the remote in his pocket, left his pillowcase, took her key ring so he could get back inside, and closed the door behind him. He was wearing a baseball cap and dark sunglasses. It wasn't his side of town, so the people he passed on the street were merely a sea of foreign faces. He made his way down to the corner of Forty-fourth and Baltimore to the pay phone. He put his quarter in the slot, dialed his number, and waited for Sticks to pick up.

"Yo, nigga, you got me, right?"

"Yeah, homie, chill, I'm there, nigga. Seven-thirty, right?" Sticks asked, confirming everything.

"Yeah, seven-thirty, the corner of Forty-third and Baltimore."

"Okay, I got you, don't worry. And look, all that paperwork you needed, I got it right here."

Nard finished talking to Sticks and hung up. He looked at his watch. *I don't know if I can wait till no seven-thirty. Damn.* Nard surveyed the block. Nothing but silence, almost too silent for West Philly. He walked back into the apartment building and took the elevator to Cathy's floor. He opened the apartment to find everything like it had been. Just as he was about to close the door behind him, he had a premonition. The police were right there, guns drawn, shouting, telling him to get on the floor, pointing loaded forty-calibers, ready to take aim and prepared to shoot to kill.

"Freeze, step away from the door, put your hands on your head." Nard turned around to see what looked like the entire police precinct in the apartment building hallway. Where they had come from, he hadn't a clue, how they got in the building he would probably never know. But one thing was for certain, they had him. He wished he could run and hide, but in his heart he knew that there was nothing more he could do.

Little did he know, he had been caught because of Cathy Robbins's bird ass. She had pretended oh so well, a real Hollywood actress, yes sir indeed. Get that bitch an Oscar now. She knew exactly what was going on when the nigga rang her phone.

"Yo, Cat, what's shaking, baby?"

"Who this, Nard?" she asked as she picked up the remote and turned down the television. She was watching Channel 10 news when the photo of Nard flashed across the screen. *I didn't know that nigga's name was no Bernard Guess.* She laughed to herself. She had been listening to Captain Dan when her phone rang. She listened to Nard with one ear and continued listening to the news with the other.

"Mmmm hmm, come right on over here. I ain't doing nothing," she said, thinking all kinds of devious thoughts to herself. "You got some condoms, right?" she asked, just to throw the nigga off. "All right then, see you in a few." Cathy jumped up off the bed memorizing the crime stoppers number. *I can't believe it, I can turn this nigga in and get me twenty-five thousand dollars. Damn, twenty-five thousand dollars just for one dumb-ass nigga. Please lord let him get here safe and sound. Let me see my crime stopper number one more time.* She looked at the piece of paper that she had written the number down on. Certain that she had the number memorized, she tore the paper into tiny pieces and threw them into the trash. And once he got there, you would never know Little Miss Crime Stopper was on her j-o-b. But she was. She pretended her ass off for that twenty-five. Fucked Nard, sucked Nard, flipped his ass all around and everything else until she could get outside to the nearest telephone booth and dial 911.

"Hello, I got him—Bernard Guess, the Somerset Killer. He's in my apartment. Hurry!"

Poor Nard, he didn't even see them coming, had no chance to even think or blink. Nard simply put his hands up and knew that this was only the beginning. Thank god, if he had nothing else at that very moment, he had an alibi.

LIAR LIAR PANTS ON FIRE

Shut the fuck up! What's his name?" Delgado asked as he looked at Ross.

"Umm, Bernard Guess," said Ross, looking in a folder at the suspect's name.

"Did we read him his rights?" asked Delgado.

"Umm, I don't know."

"Exactly. How the fuck you going to arrest me and not read me my rights."

"Shut the fuck up!" said Delgado, as he punched Nard hard in his face. "You don't have any rights; fucking read him his rights," ordered Delgado.

Ross began reading his rights to him as she looked at her chipped pointer fingernail.

"Anything you say can and will be used against you. You have the right to an attorney. If you cannot afford one, one will be appointed for you," she said. She bit her nail, then continued.

"I need my phone call."

"The lines must be down, phones not working," she said as she spat her fingernail in his direction, lifted the phone, listened to the dial tone, then hung it back up.

"Who the fuck are you calling?"

"I don't have to answer any of your questions," said Nard, already knowing his rights.

"Shut the fuck up!" said Delgado, sucker-punching Nard and watching him fall out of the chair and onto the floor.

Merva glanced up but simply continued reading Nard his Miranda rights.

"Stop hitting me, fuck is wrong with you."

"What the fuck is wrong with you? You want to tell me what happened on Somerset and why you killed those people?"

"Fuck outta here. I ain't killed nobody."

"Really, you didn't kill a little boy?"

"No."

"Shut the fuck up, fucking liar," said Tommy. He hit Nard so hard that he lay, eyes wide open, unconscious on the floor.

"See, how we gonna interrogate him if you gonna beat the suspect up?" said Ross, looking at her partner.

"I fucking hate being lied to, Merva, it fucking pisses me off," said Tommy as he sniffled and wiped his nose.

"There's a bug going around."

"I know. I got the worst cold."

"Try TheraFlu."

"Aargh, my head," said Nard, looking around the room.

"Get the fuck up and stop acting like you're hurt. I want to know what happened and why you killed those people. And if you don't stop playing games with me, I'm going to sit you in a holding cell until you're ready to talk."

"I told you, I don't know nothing about no murders. I was in the Honey Dipper that night. I was drinking and partying with some girl. I think her name was Rose, no, no, it was Daisy."

"Don't fucking lie to me, I swear to god, don't fucking lie to me, pal."

"I'm not lying. I swear, I was in the Honey Dipper. I ain't killed nobody," said Nard with extreme confidence. "You better check my alibi."

"I'm not checking jack shit, pal. Fuck you and fuck what you said. You were already picked by your victim, bro. Book him on murder one, fucking slime bag. Get him the fuck outta here," said Delgado, shooing Nard away from him.

"Book him?" asked the officer.

"Yup, book him. Lock his ass up until the cows come home for all I care."

"He's lying. You know he's lying about his alibi," Merva said, looking at Tommy, who was shaking his head, ready to blow a gasket.

"Of course he is. Saunta Davis IDed this scumbag before she died. I'm not letting this guy go. He's a murderer and he's the one, I know he is. I can feel it. He killed those people, Ross, he killed them."

"I know, Delgado, calm down, we got our killer."

Reggie pulled his sleek and sexy Jaguar to a complete stop in front of a For Sale sign that had been placed on a perfectly land-scaped lawn.

"I rode by this house yesterday. Don't you love it?" he asked as he grabbed her hand.

"Oh, my god, Reggie, yes. It's . . ." She just couldn't find the words. ". . . absolutely the most beautiful house I've ever seen."

"I know, and look, it has a fenced-in backyard, so it probably has a pool, too. I think we should definitely put this on our list of homes to see. This is a good neighborhood, with good schools, and it's real close to the city. I like Mount Airy, don't you?"

"I love it; I could live here," said Daisy, all smiles.

"So, you call the agent and ask her the price and set up a time for her to show you some houses in the neighborhood, but start with this one. Then when I get back from this business trip I got to take, you can give me a full report."

"You leaving? When you coming back?"

"I got to go out the country to take care of some business, but I'll be back in two weeks. Don't worry, I'll be back, and when I get back I'll need to know everything, from how old the house is, to how many bedrooms and how many baths it has, but the most important thing is that you like it, and you'll be happy living in it."

She looked at Reggie and at that moment she knew she had found the man of her dreams. He was someone who would look out for her and take care of her and be a good provider to her. He was the perfect height, nice and tall just the way she thought the man of her dreams would be. And while he dressed in suits, he was very down to earth. Reggie was five-eleven and weighed in at 213 pounds. He was a tad on the heavy side, carrying a few pounds that he had put on over the past couple of years, but all in all, he carried the weight just fine. He was a handsome man, very appealing, with dark brown eyes, black hair, and a smile that would warm your heart.

"Reggie, I'm happy just being with you."

"Me too, baby. I got to go by the shoe store right quick, and then I'll drop you off, okay?"

Daisy figured that now was a better time than any to tell Reggie about her losing her job. Well, she wouldn't actually be telling him about her real job, but she would pretend that her make-pretend job was her real job, and real or fake she didn't have it anymore. Worst thing was that she didn't have any income. She was praying deep down in her bones that the man of her dreams would help her with her rent. Lord knows she'd need it now that she had no job.

"Umm, there's something I need to tell you, Reggie," said Daisy as she looked down at her hands folded in her lap.

"What, babe, why you looking like that for?"

" 'Cause I lost my job."

"You lost your job? What happened?"

"They said that business was slow and they couldn't afford to keep me, so they had to let me go," she said, trying to look and sound as convincing as possible.

"Damn, baby, I'm sorry to hear that. Don't worry about it, you'll get another job."

"I know, it's just that I don't know what I'm going to do until then. I don't know how I'm gonna pay my rent."

"Don't worry about it. I got you, you're my girl, so you ain't got nothing to worry about."

Daisy just sat back in the luxury of the Jaguar and looked out the window as the car rolled past the city streets. People waiting for buses, nope that wasn't her, and young mothers pushing strollers, nope that wasn't her, old people limping down the streets holding canes in their hands, that wouldn't be her. No, Daisy had plans, big plans, and because of Reggie Carter all her dreams were beginning to come true, or at least that's what she thought.

The next morning Daisy woke and got out of bed. She felt an undescribable soreness and when she tried to use the bathroom, an undescribable burning sensation. The burning and soreness were so bad that she immediately called her doctor and made an emergency appointment. Just as she opened the door and was about to leave, the mailman entered the vestibule, unlocked the mail holder caddy, and began placing everyone's mail in their caddy holders.

"Here you go," he said as he handed the day's mail to Daisy.

"Thanks," she said, turning around and taking the mail back inside her apartment. In too much of a rush to get to the doctor's office, she threw the mail on the kitchen table and walked back out of the apartment, locking the door behind her.

Dr. Vistane's office was located at Thirty-eighth and Lancaster. A clinic well known for performing abortions and counseling young pregnant teens, it sat right on the corner. Daisy signed in and let the receptionist know that she was there for an emergency visit. After thirty minutes of waiting, Daisy heard her name being called. She was taken upstairs, and after a nurse took her weight, temperature, and blood pressure, she was placed in a room, given a plastic cup, and told to give a urine sample. Then she was to undress completely below the waist, lie on the table, and cover up with a paper covering. A few minutes later Dr. Vistane came into the room. He spoke with Daisy about how she was feeling and upon examination told Daisy to dress and that he'd be back in a few minutes, after testing some culture samples.

It turned out that there were quite a few diagnoses made that day.

"Daisy, you're having what we consider to be a herpes initial outbreak."

"What?"

"You have contracted the herpes virus, and the soreness and burning sensation are a result of the initial outbreak. It's right at the tip of the opening of your vagina. It's going to be painful and sore for at least the next three to possibly five days. After which it will form a scab and disappear. Usually, patients will have their initial outbreak and . . ." The doctor looked up from his chart to find Daisy in a pool of tears.

"Herpes?" she asked.

"Yes, Daisy, I am sorry."

"But how? When? I don't understand."

"Well, sometimes it can be hard to pinpoint when, but the virus can lie dormant. Medically, they say anywhere from two to twenty days, even sometimes longer once you've been exposed to the virus. And your outbreak can last for several weeks. Once the outbreak heals, the virus will lie dormant in your nervous system until it re-emerges and you have your next outbreak, which could be one month from now or twenty years from now. Stop crying, this isn't the end of the world. Millions of people are diagnosed with this virus, and after they're diagnosed, some never have a recurrence again; others do. Daisy, it's not the end of the world."

Daisy's mind scrambled. *Lies dormant for weeks, may or may not come back again. There's no telling who passed this to me.* Thirty days. She had slept with twenty or so men in the last thirty days alone. *What the fuck am I going to do now?*

"When is the last time you had intercourse?"

She couldn't help but think of nasty Felix and the last time she was at the Honey Pot, and how Calvin fired her and then she went home and had sex with Reggie, and then had sex with Reggie practically every day thereafter. *Oh, my god, what if I've given him herpes too. What if he has it now. Oh my god, if I done gave him this herpes virus, he'll kill me, just kill me. What am I going to do? I can't tell him, I can't tell anybody.* Daisy wasn't even listening to the doctor. She was too preoccupied with her own thoughts, trying to figure out who had burned her and passed her this horrid, dreaded virus. Not to mention, her mind was swirling with the thought that she had passed the virus on to Reggie, and lord only knew what would happen, and the worst of it all was that he'd probably never speak to her again.

"So, I want to start you on some medication. You take it by mouth twice a day. And here's a prescription for some ointment. It will help with the burning and itching you may have. Now, on a lighter side, you also have trichomoniasis."

"Trick-a-what?" she said, looking at the doctor as if she couldn't take any more diagnoses.

"It's vaginal bacteria, also transmitted sexually. You really need to be careful with trichomoniasis because once we treat you, if you have sex with an infected person who has not been treated you will catch the bacteria again. It's really important that we get your partner treated."

Reggie has trichomoniasis; I can't tell him that. I gave it to him.

He'll kill me if I tell him, and probably hate me, but definitely never want to be with me again.

The doctor watched as she sat silent and still. Dr. Vistane wasn't sure if she was even hearing him.

"Even if you're not going to have sex with him again, he needs to know that he has had exposure to the bacteria and possibly the herpes virus."

"I can't believe this," said Daisy, as the doctor continued to explain the diagnosis. "Are you sure?"

"Yes, I'm positive. So, if you can make a list for me, I will contact all the people that you have been in contact with."

A list. I'd be here all night and day. No, we ain't doing no lists, that's on them. They'll figure it out, just like I did, sitting in the clinic.

"Um, no, I don't know how to contact the guy," Daisy lied.

"It was only one guy that you've been sexually active with in the last thirty to forty-five days?"

"Yes, just one guy," said Daisy, lying through her teeth, as she wiped her tears from her eyes.

"Okay, wait . . ." said Dr. Vistane as he saw Daisy getting up from the table. "I'm not done yet."

"There's more?" asked Daisy.

"Yeah, there's more," said Dr. Vistane, shaking his head yes and looking as if he hated to be the bearer of all this bad news. "You are pregnant."

"Pregnant?"

"Yup, by the looks of it, six weeks," said Dr. Vistane.

"Pregnant?"

"I take it this is an unwanted pregnancy?" asked Dr. Vistane.

"Yes, I can't believe it . . . I just can't believe it. I'm on the pill, though," she said, knowing that there had to be some kind of medical mistake.

"I understand, but the pill is only 99 percent effective. There are those, like you, who unfortunately are that pregnant one percent. Would you like to come in and speak to one of the nurses about pregnancy counseling or other possible alternatives?"

Daisy couldn't believe it. Not another abortion. She herself didn't know if she could take another one; the sound of the machine alone terrified her. *There has to be another way.*

"Daisy, would you like counseling?"

"Yes, I want an abortion. I don't want this baby. I want an abortion."

"Are you sure?"

"I'm positive, just please, Dr. Vistane, please make the appointment for me."

"Okay, no problem. I'll take care of everything. Come on, stop crying. Everything is going to be okay now. You'll be just fine, Daisy, just fine. I'll take good care of you."

Detective Honing and Detective Walters sat in the Honey Dipper looking every bit like needles in a haystack.

"Can I get another?" asked Honing, realizing a new waitress was serving him.

"Whatchoo drinking?"

"Um, Coke," said Honing, unable to take his eyes off her perfect double Ds.

"Wow," said Walters as he looked the waitress up and down. "This is fucking torture, man. I love it though. I swear my wife is really in for it when I get home tonight."

"Oh, yeah, well one of these broads is in for it right here, right now, when I get off work," said Honing, wishing he could tear the waitress's back out.

"Hey, there he is," the waitress said, as the detectives looked over their backs to the front doorway. "Hey, Calvin, these gentlemen are here to see you," she said as she walked away to the other end of the bar.

"What can I do for ya?" asked Calvin, looking at the police officers and wondering what in the world they were doing there. He had enough shit going on, he didn't need any more, and he certainly didn't need the police in his spot.

"Umm, is there somewhere we can go and talk that might have a little more privacy?" asked Detective Walters.

"Why, we can't talk right here?" asked Calvin, as if he had nothing to hide.

"Well, we're investigating the Somerset killings. I don't know if you heard about them in the news?" said Honing.

"Yeah, but what's that got to do with me?" asked Calvin, sounding like a song.

"Well, it turns out that the suspect claims he was in your establishment here on the night in question. He claims he was with one of your dancers, a girl by the name of Daisy. Do you have any dancers here by that name? We'd like to speak with her," finished Honing.

Calvin looked up at the double D waitress all in his conversation, listening to every word the detectives spoke.

"Umm, why don't you follow me back here to my office where we can get a little more privacy," said Calvin. "Go on, get back to work before I five your ass, nosy-ass broads in here," said Calvin, holding up his hand like he was Ike Turner or somebody.

"I ain't late, five your damn self," mumbled Tina, looking at Calvin and wondering where he got his nerve.

Calvin took the police into the back where the vultures couldn't watch them like they were roadkill.

"So, you say that Somerset Killer claims he was here, huh?" said Calvin, smelling a big, stinky rat.

"Yeah, that's his alibi, he was here in your bar with your dancer, Daisy. Here let me show you his photo and maybe you can see if you recognize him."

Walters pulled out a mug shot, handed it to Calvin, and carefully watched his expression. His face was completely empty. The photo meant nothing to him, the face meant nothing to him, and the god's honest truth was he had never seen the man in his life.

"Nope, never seen him before," said Calvin, passing the photo back. He walked over to the far left side of the room where he had several file cabinets, opened the drawer, and pulled out the folder on Daisy Mae Fothergill.

"Here you go. She don't work here no more, but you more than welcome to look at the information here in the folder. That should answer all your questions about her, but as you can see, she quit about three weeks ago."

"You haven't seen her?"

"Nope, I haven't heard a word from her."

"Do you mind?" asked Honing, reaching for a piece of blank paper on Calvin's desk.

"Help yourself."

Calvin stood patiently as the detectives went through his employment folder on Daisy. They got what they came for. They knew exactly who she was, right on down to her Social Security number, address, and birth date.

"I think that will be all for now. However, we have to ask that you not leave town."

"Can't leave town? Why, I'm not a suspect, am I?"

"No, sir, but while we are investigating we might need you here for questioning, that's all. Contact me directly if you plan on leaving the city, okay?" asked Walters, handing him his police precinct card.

Calvin took the card and his employment folder on Daisy and placed the card inside the folder. He set the folder on his desk and escorted the detectives back out the door.

"Thanks for your assistance. You've been a big help," said Honing.

"Yeah, no problem, any time," said Calvin as he turned back into his office. He closed the door, went over to his desk. He looked inside Daisy's folder at the detective's card; Homicide division. *Smells like a rat to me. What mess you done got yourself into now, Daisy?*

JACKPOT

So what's the lawyer saying?" asked Sticks as he spoke to Nard through the plate glass, using a black telephone that had no dialing pad, just the handset hanging from the wall.

"Man, he's saying that it looks good, real good, but he needs to talk to that chick, from the Honey Dipper, what's her name? Daisy, right?"

"Yeah, Daisy. So the lawyer wants to speak with her?"

"Yeah, he said he needs to prep her for her testimony and shit," said Nard as he looked down at the floor.

"What?" asked Sticks.

"Man, this shit got me fucked up. I don't know how long I can hold up. They got a nigga in a fucking cell, man. And I ain't never been locked up in my life. This shit ain't cool," said Nard, looking at Sticks and wishing he was a free man.

"Listen, everything's going to be all right, just get me the name of the lawyer and I'll get the girl and take her down there. Don't worry, they can only hold you for six months, then they got to go to trial since they not giving you no bail."

"Yeah, the lawyer said he's going in front of the judge next week to see if he can get them to consider bail, but then he's saying if he does get bail, it'll be so high, won't nobody be able to pay it."

"Well, even if they don't give you bail, you outta here in six months and that's nothing. You can do it. Trust me, six months is nothing. That shit will be over in no time."

Sticks got a piece of paper and a pen from a guard and wrote down Nard's lawyer's information. "Don't worry, baby boy, I got you covered." With that, Sticks put his fist to the glass and waited for Nard to return the pound. It was hard to see a brother behind bars, real hard, especially for Sticks, 'cause he had been in and out of prison since he was thirteen years old, so he knew how them white folks got down with their penal institutions and rehabilitation programs. Most important though, he knew what it felt like to be locked in a cage and he knew how lonely it could be. He walked a little faster just thinking about it. *They not locking me up again. I'd rather die first*, he thought to himself. *Nard got to stay focused and not let them walls get him trapped.* It sounded simple, but it wasn't. Sticks knew they were constantly interrogating Nard, trying to get him to mess up his words or, worst case, snitch on someone. And that was the last thing he wanted, because deep down inside he knew if Nard did turn state, he'd turn on him, and between the possibility of prison and the possibility of Simon Shuller's eating his ass alive, he saw his only option as doing the right thing and helping out a friend. He had to make sure Nard was straight. He had no choice.

* * *

It had been over a week since Reggie had left for his business trip. He told her he would try to call, but so far she hadn't heard from him. She had contacted the real estate office and found out the price of the home they looked at. The sellers were asking for $425,000. Reggie said anything she liked priced under half a million they should look at, so she had an appointment for later today to see the place. Still though, she wished he would call. Every night before she went to bed she dialed his cell phone, but the call would go straight to voicemail and she'd listen to his sexy voice talking to her, telling her to leave a message. She never did though. Once the message was over, she'd just hang up the phone. Just then her phone rang. *Reggie.* She just knew it was him. She answered the phone with sheer excitement in her voice.

"Yo, where you been?" the voice asked calmly.

"Who is this?" responded Daisy, a little disappointed that the voice on the other end of the line wasn't Reggie.

"Damn, you forget about me already? It's Sticks."

Sticks? What the fuck do this nigga want? He ain't been bothering to call me. He must want something.

"You got some nerve calling me. You know Trixie still ain't speaking to me. That shit you did to me was real fucked up too. And then y'all left us. We didn't have no way to get home or nothing," said Daisy, thinking of the night she and Trixie did a party for Sticks. Both girls had been drugged with gamma-hydroxybutyrate acid, known in the streets as GHB. They had been raped and even sodomized, but worst of all, they hadn't been paid.

"Look, man, that's the past, don't even worry about that shit. I'm sorry. It won't happen again."

You can bet your bottom dollar it won't. "Well, thanks for the apology. So, what's going on?"

"Nothing, man, I got to come and get you."

"Come get me for what?"

"We gonna go see that lawyer."

"Lawyer, what lawyer?"

"For my man, the one you gave the alibi for, remember?"

Daisy had almost forgotten about that statement she had given to the private investigator Sticks had sent to her house. It had been three, maybe four months ago and for her that was like a lifetime.

"Yeah, but what's that got to do with a lawyer?" she asked, not getting the gist of the mess she had gotten herself into for a measly two thousand dollars.

"You got to go to court, so the lawyer wants to prepare you."

"Go to court? I ain't going to no court."

"Yo, Dais, stop playing. You got to testify. You gave Nard the alibi. You said he was with you, that's what you told the investigator, and the investigator gave his report to Nard's lawyer, so Nard's lawyer needs to prepare you for trial. Yo, why you bugging?"

Bugging, did he ask me why I'm bugging? Is he fucking crazy? He's the one bugging.

"Wait, wait, wait, you ain't tell me all this. You never told me all this. You told me to just give that statement to a private investigator. You ain't say nothing about no lawyers or having to go to court. Shit, you the one that's bugging."

"Yo, Dais, look, man, I got you, whatever you want just name it."

Well, now his ass is talking. "You don't want me to start naming. I got a list longer than your arm of shit I need over here."

"All right, then so put the list together and I'll be over there to get you at say two o'clock."

"No I can't, not today," she said, thinking of her realtor meeting. *Fuck, I need to get me some money from Sticks while he talking my kinda talk. Maybe I should cancel with the house. No, let me do the house.* "Yeah, we got to do this tomorrow or something."

"Man, Dais, you fucking up, man. Listen, this shit is getting ready to get serious. You gonna have to be on call and ready to rock and roll, dig me."

"Yeah, I dig you, but me and my boyfriend is buying me a house and I got shit to do."

"You got a man?"

"Yeah, and he's buying me a house. That's why I'm saying all this court shit ain't cool and you calling ain't cool either."

"Listen, this court shit is your duty, you been paid and like I just said, you do what the fuck you're suppose to and just get me the list of everything you need and I got you. You take care of me, I take care of you. You got it."

"Yeah, Sticks, I got it."

"All right, I'll call you back and let you know when we going to the lawyer's office. Don't have nothing to do either, no more excuses, and boyfriend or not when I see you I'm tapping that ass, you understand. You know who the fuck I am, dammit."

"Yeah, Sticks, whatever you say," said Daisy, a little agitated.

I don't know who he thinks he is but he ain't tapping nothing here. He really got some nerve.

I don't know who this bitch thinks she's talking to, but if she don't get that alibi straight with Nard's lawyer that bitch is gonna find herself never speaking again. Sticks hung up the phone with a bad feeling. *She's going to be a problem. I can just feel it.*

He wondered would she come through for him with the alibi. If she didn't, Simon Shuller would have his and Nard's asses in a sling and Sticks knew it. But for Daisy it was too late. She had to come through with the alibi, either that or she'd be in the same sling as Nard and Sticks, but unfortunately for her, she didn't know she had gotten herself in bed with a member of the mafia and was the alibi witness for the Somerset Killer.

That afternoon Daisy went looking at all the homes for sale that the realtor had on her list. They must have visited eleven properties in one afternoon. Daisy made notes, asked lots of questions about each listing, and fell in love with every house she walked into. It was unbelievable, dynamic views, open space, large kitchens with eat-ins, master bedrooms with walk-in closets, fireplaces, master bathrooms with oversized Jacuzzis, kitchens with granite countertops and stainless-steel appliance packages, marble foyers, and two- and three-car garages. Daisy couldn't believe that people actually lived in homes that beautiful. She rode by this kind of home every day, but had no idea how people were living inside of them.

"So, did you see anything you like?"

"I sure did, and I can't wait to show Reggie. I just know he's going to love them."

"Any one in particular caught your eye?"

"You know, actually, yes, the third house and the eighth house. I really like them, a lot, and I can't wait to show my fiancé as soon as he gets back. I just know he's going to love them," said Daisy, before thanking the agent and parting ways.

That night she went home and as usual she tried to call Reggie, but instead of his answering machine, she got something different—that universal operator that advises you that the number you have dialed has been changed, has been disconnected, or is no longer in service. Daisy figured she had dialed the wrong number and tried again, but got the same message. *Why is his phone off? Maybe he didn't pay the bill before he went out of town. Yeah, that's it, he probably didn't pay the bill.*

It had been three weeks, three long, drawn-out, stressful weeks of no Reggie. The number was still disconnected, he hadn't called, he hadn't come back. He had said he would only be gone for a week or two, but it had been longer, and her heart began to grow heavier and heavier. Every time the phone rang, it was Sticks. *What the fuck do he want now?* She had gone down to the lawyer's office like he asked, but it turned out that the lawyer had another matter pop up, had to go out of town, and had put Nard's case on the back burner after getting several extensions filed with the court. Nard didn't know what was going on and was a nervous wreck. He was calling Sticks's phone more than a young Puerto Rican girl in heat. *Fuck, what's he want now?* Sticks had to take his call. God forbid he not answer and the nigga turn state. No, whenever Nard called, Sticks made sure he answered.

Just then a loud knock at Daisy's door, more of a banging, rang out through the apartment.

"Who is it?" she hollered at the door.

"It's the police, open up."

The police, the police? What the hell are they doing here? What do they want from me?

Tommy Delgado watched as the door opened and a young girl with long hair and green eyes stared back at him. "Can I help you?"

"Yeah, I hope so. I'm looking for Daisy M. Fothergill."

"I'm Daisy."

"Do you mind if we come in?" said Delgado, smiling, with Merva standing behind him grinning even harder.

"Umm, I guess so, sure."

"We're only going to need a few minutes of your time," said Ross, her smile fading quickly. "We're investigating the murders of Ponado Fernandez, Jeremy Tyler, and Lance Robertson," she said, watching Daisy like a hawk, looking for any sign that Daisy was lying to them.

"What's that got to do with me? I never heard of them people."

"Well, let me tell you, the man that has been identified as the Somerset Killer and killed these people," said Delgado, spreading crime-scene photos of the Three Musketeers lying in pools of blood, "claims that he was with you the night in question. And I got to tell you, I find it really hard to believe."

"Why is that?" asked Daisy nervously.

"I'll tell you why. He killed a nine-year-old boy and shot up his mother and right before she died, she identified Bernard Guess from a series of photos. Now, I got an open-and-shut case, everything from fingerprints on down to a positive ID, but then I get a report from Mr. Guess's lawyer claiming you're their star witness and my Somerset Killer was with you the night in question at the Honey Dipper and therefore couldn't possibly have been on the 2500 block of Somerset when the murders occurred."

Delgado stopped and waited to see what her response was to all of that, and unfortunately she had none.

"So, about that night, do you think you could answer some questions for me?" asked Delgado, trying to figure her out.

"What kind of questions?"

"Just general, like what time did Mr. Guess come into the bar on November 5?"

"Umm, I don't remember what time he got there," she answered.

"Do you remember what he was wearing?" asked Merva.

"No, I don't."

"Was he alone?" she followed up.

"Yes, I think so," Daisy said, wishing she had never let them in her house.

"You think so—don't you know?" asked Merva.

"Yeah, I think he was alone," said Daisy, trying to sound convincing.

"What was he drinking that night?"

"Umm . . ." Daisy sat still for a few seconds, acting as if she was really trying to think hard. "You know what, I don't really remember that either," said Daisy, wishing Sticks or somebody had prepped her. And the bad thing was, she had let them in. *What was I thinking. Next time we talk outside. These guys are really getting comfortable and they're asking me all these questions. I don't even know what this guy looks like.*

"Are you sure you remember him there?" asked Merva, starting not to believe this girl one bit.

"Yeah, he was there. It was just so long ago, you know."

"Do you still work at the Honey Dipper?" asked Delgado. "I swear you look like I've seen you somewhere before."

Daisy giggled, but honestly had never seen him in her life. "No, not no more. I was working at the Honey Pot, but I quit working there about a month ago."

"Why?" asked Ross, being a little nosy.

"I just wanted to do something else, you know. It gets hard after a while, or at least for me it did."

"How long have you been dancing, in places . . . like that?" asked Delgado, trying not to use descriptive vocabulary. Detective Ross immediately looked at him and quickly interceded.

"Yeah, Daisy, how long have you been a stripper?" said Ross, looking over at Delgado. *What the fuck is he doing, trying to be nice to her? She's lying through her teeth and he's showing her mercy. What's wrong with him?*

"Umm . . ."

"Don't tell me you don't know that either," said Ross sarcastically, tired of playing games with Daisy. She was ready to take her in, sit her in a room, and leave her there for maybe two or three days and then see if her memory got any better, and that was exactly what she planned on doing.

"No, I know when I started dancing, it was like four years ago, after I turned eighteen," said Daisy with an ounce of confidence.

"So, you're only twenty-two years old?" asked Ross, as Daisy shook her head yes. "I think we need to take her downtown for questioning," Ross advised, looking over at Delgado, who seemed to be admiring the young girl, not taking his eyes off her for one second. "What do you think?" she asked, wondering why he wasn't responding. She looked again and he was still staring intensely.

"No, I don't think we should take her downtown. I think we should give her a chance to think about what she's doing. Have you thought about what you're doing, Daisy?" asked Tommy, knowing exactly what was going on. She was being used for an alibi. She wasn't a real alibi.

"I don't understand what you mean."

"Okay, let me explain to you," said Delgado.

Ross interrupted. "No, let me explain," she said, stepping in front of Tommy, who had really pissed her off, with his "No, I don't think we should take her downtown" bull crap.

"Let me be clear with you. These three men were murdered. This mother and her son were murdered, and you need to look at them really, really good, because not only are you lying to investigators, you're lying to me! And the guy who killed them needs to be brought down, and your little daydream story you got going is going to crash all around you, and when it does, I'll be there and I'll be charging you with everything from perjury to obstructing justice, do you got that? 'Cause when I'm done with you, you'll be figuring out everything that you don't know in a nice comfy cell inside Muncy. So, you just think about that, because if you keep fucking around with me that's right where you'll be! You got that, Honey Dipper?" asked Merva, leaning over the table, her hands on the table supporting her weight as she bent down in Daisy's face.

"Okay," called out Tommy as Merva stared Daisy eye to eye before backing up off her. "We will need you to come down to the Thirty-second Precinct. You might want to get a lawyer and have him present when you come in. Call me tomorrow, and we can set up a time for you, okay?" asked Delgado. He felt really bad. She was going to make a horrible witness, probably end up perjuring herself under oath and end up in prison just like Ross said.

PAYIN' THE PIPER

Yo, Daisy, open this god damn door!" yelled Lester Giles, the owner of the building, better known as her "straight from the depths of hell" landlord. "I know you in there."

Daisy couldn't take the pounding on her door any longer. "What?" she said, agitated, as she flung the chain off the door, unlocked the deadbolt, and pulled the door open.

"What? You asking me what? I know you ain't getting nasty. You got my rent money? That's what."

"Look, Lester, I just need one more week, please. I'm waiting for my boyfriend to get back and once he get here I'll have that for you."

"You say what, again?" he asked, making her repeat herself. "Is you out your god damn mind? I ain't waiting on no nigga, is you crazy? You sitting here waiting on a nigga. Shit, you might as well get to stepping to the nearest homeless shelter and wait on this motherfucker over there. But not here. What is you doing? You ain't even working no more."

"How you know what I'm doing?" asked Daisy, frowning up at him.

"Don't worry about that, I need my money, that's what you gots to be worried about, rent." Then he spelled it out for her. "Ah-ra, eeee, annnn, teeeee! Now, you gots my money or not, and don't play with me."

"Lester, come on, please, seriously. Don't I always pay you? Come on, I always take care of you. Don't I?"

"Then you gonna have to take some caring tonight, baby. Whoo whee, just rock my world. You sure is pretty, you know that, don'tcha?" he said, reaching up and rubbing his finger across her face and then down on her titty.

"Lester, stop playing," she said, knocking his hand down.

"Girl, you think I'm playing with you. I'll throw you and everything you got out on the street tonight. You understand, Daisy," he said in an evil whisper. "Now what you gonna do?" he said, sneering at her like the grim reaper and meaning every word he spoke.

It wouldn't be the first time she had had to give Lester Giles sexual services to keep a roof over her head. All she could do was pray that it would be the last. She thought of Reggie. *Damn, I wish I didn't have to. But, what he don't know, won't hurt him.* She hated it, hated the thought of it. She really loved Reggie and wanted their sex to be sacred, cherishable, and not tainted by someone else. Not to mention that she hated Lester. He was dark-skinned, but you could still see a long scar on the left side of his face. He had a bushy afro of dusty gray hair and the hugest potbelly you could imagine. *Reggie, where are you? If only you could just step right off that elevator right now and save me.* She looked at the elevator door, realizing it was merely wishful thinking. She opened her apartment door so that Lester could pass by.

"That's what I thought," he said as she closed the door and watched him begin to massage himself.

A couple hours later, after she had satisfied her rent debt, Daisy sat in her living room alone. She turned on the television, but her mind was heavy. She didn't really watch the TV, just sat still. The phone rang. She looked at it, but didn't answer it. She knew who it was, *Sticks*. As much as she wanted to answer it, in anticipation of Reggie's possibly calling, she didn't answer it. She already knew it wasn't him. She just had a horrible feeling he was gone. *I can't believe Reggie left me like that. What did I do? I don't understand. Maybe I should go to his mother's house.* It was very far away, somewhere out in Montgomery County on the other side of City Line Avenue. She didn't even know if she would be able to find her way back there. And Sticks wasn't really asking her to do anything, he was more or less telling her what she was gonna do. *He's really ordering me around, and the police, they know I'm lying.* Poor Daisy, if there was one thing she wasn't good at, it was lying. She had tried her best, but she knew in her heart that the cops were looking in her eyes reading the truth. *What am I going to do? She said I'll be in Muncy for perjury, and that poor little boy. Why'd he kill them people like that?* It was too much, not to mention she was flat broke. Daisy looked in her pocketbook and took out her wallet. She flashed through the bills—sixty-seven dollars and some loose change. That wasn't much when that was all you had to your name, with nothing and nobody to help you. *What am I going to do?* She thought about it, hard. *Sticks did say to make a list of things I needed.* Truth was, Sticks was going to have to do something; he was all she had to help her out. *I better go back to the Honey Pot and get Calvin to give me my job back, and I know he's gonna make me beg like a dog for it, too. But what else can I do? I ain't got no choice.* And truth was, she really didn't, she had nothing and had no one. *Love sure don't love nobody. How could I be so stupid.*

She hopped up, got dressed, and made her way down to the Honey Dipper. By the time she got there it was almost midnight, and that was perfect timing to catch Calvin in his office.

She walked inside. Saying hello to familiar faces, she made her way to the bar.

"Damn, Daisy Mae, I almost ain't recognize you with your clothes on. Shit, how you been?" asked Dallas, happy to see her.

"Oh, I been okay. Got so much going on, you know?"

"Man, do I, it's been rough for everybody though. Just got to hang in there."

"Yup, just gotta hang in there. Hey, Dallas, where's Calvin?" asked Daisy, cool, calm, and collected.

"He's back there in his office."

"Oh, 'cause I really need to see him."

"Well, be careful, he might not recognize you with them clothes on." Dallas laughed to himself as Daisy made her way to the back of the club where Calvin's office was.

"Who is it?" he growled from behind his desk.

"It's me," said Daisy as she peeked from behind the door and let herself in.

"What in the world do you want now?"

"Listen, Calvin, I'm sorry."

"Sorry, you damn right you sorry. You got the god damn police all over this motherfucker. Everywhere you turn there they are. I can't keep no business in here and it's all because of you. I don't know what the fuck is wrong with you girls. You stupid or something? You can't think? All you good for is lying on your backs and opening your legs. That's it! Get on out of here; ain't nothing I can do for you," said Calvin with blistering coldness.

"Calvin, please, I came back to work, I'm not trying to cause no trouble."

"Work, girl, is you crazy? Let me tell you something, these god damn police is talking about some minor was in my bar on November 5 and was with you drinking. They threatening to close me down, and I swear I won't lose my business behind your stinkin' ass. You hear me, Daisy, I won't, god damn it. Whatever you done told them police or whoever, you better think again, 'cause if they subpoena me to come to court, I'm telling 'em that you wasn't even working that night. Shit, you think you gonna close me down? Is you out your fucking mind? Get the fuck outta here, Daisy. I don't want to see you no more. You nothing but trouble, nothing but trouble."

"I'm sorry Calvin, I didn't me—"

"Don't matter what you meant, only matters what you do, and you doing some fucked-up shit, for some real fucked-up people. You better be careful or you gonna wind up in an alleyway somewhere dead," said Calvin, as he watched Daisy close the door behind her.

"That's right, get on outta here, talking about some god damn Bernard Guess in this motherfucker, nigga ain't even old enough to piss straight, let alone drink, and he in this motherfucker fucking my shit up for me. I don't think so," said Calvin, hot and bothered, and needing something or somebody to cool him off. He peeked out his door.

"Hey, Cherry Tree, come on in here," said Calvin, grabbing a half-naked cocktail waitress by the arm.

"My name is Cherry Blossom," the girl said, as if Calvin really needed to get it right.

"Aaww, shit, Cherry Tree, Cherry Blossom, shit's all the same, you just get on in here."

If nothing else, owning a strip club had its membership rewards, and every now and then, Calvin would cash them in. It was rare, but every blue moon, he took full advantage of being the boss.

Daisy went home realizing that the situation that she thought was bad with Sticks was actually worse than she had imagined. *Why the fuck would he want an alibi for someone in a bar that wasn't old enough to drink? This nigga got me all in the middle of some real bullshit. I can't even get my job back with Calvin. I ain't got no money. The police is talking about locking my ass up in Muncy and this nigga is threatening me to say this bullshit alibi. Is he nuts?* Daisy honestly didn't know what to do. All she knew was that she was beginning to wish she had never given that alibi statement to that investigator. *Oh, Momma, if only I had listened to you.* She had no idea that one alibi statement would end up costing her for the rest of her life.

It was almost two o'clock in the morning by the time she got back home. She was hungry and tired. There was a corner left in a box of Cap'n Crunch cereal. She poured some milk into the bowl and sat down at the kitchen table. *Look at that pile of mail. I bet it's all bills in there.* Sometimes, the realities of life can make you afraid, and that's what Daisy was feeling just looking at the mail. *I ain't got no money to pay no bills. They're gonna cut the phone off.* She started by opening up an AT&T envelope. And sure enough, it was a cut-off notice. *Cut it off, the only mother- fucker calling is that damn Sticks and I sure as hell don't want to talk to him no way.* She still couldn't believe that Reggie had broke out on her, with no plans to return. *I just can't believe it. I know he's coming back, he's got to come back.*

Daisy sat there opening up each envelope, looking at the total due boxes. *Mmm, no television, 'cause won't be no cable. Damn, the lights too. I better find some candles. Shit, I'm liable to be sitting here in the god damn dark any second now. This is crazy.* There was an envelope marked Abigail Fothergill. It was her mother's bank statement. She opened it and glanced at the pages, put it back in the envelope, and laid it on the table. *Wait, what the . . .* She picked the envelope back up, pulled the state- ment out again, and looked at the bottom right-hand corner, at the total. *It must be some kind of mistake, some kind of big mistake.* There was $47,422.04 in her dead mother's bank account, and she was named as a cosigner on the account.

She looked closer at the statement, and approximately three and a half weeks ago, there was a fifty-thousand dollar de- posit made, a debit of $2,577.96, and a remaining balance of $47,422.04. *Oh, my god, it must be some kind of bank error. But, what if . . . what if that money is still sitting there? What if the bank hasn't realized they made a mistake? Oh, my god, please let that money still be there.* Just then Daisy's phone rang. *Go ahead, Sticks, I'm counting money over here, nigga. I ain't got time for you and your fake ass, ain't gonna work, alibi. Shit, a bitch got money to spend and shit.* Daisy was suddenly sparked by the thought of all that money really being there. So sparked that she sat up all night long, dancing, prancing, talking to herself in the mirror, and ignoring her ringing phone.

The next morning, Daisy was standing on the corner of Thirty-eighth and Chestnut streets waiting for the bank to open. The lettering on the glass window of the bank said it opened at eight-thirty. Daisy glanced at her watch. All right now, it was eight-thirty. *Come on, what's the holdup.* Patience was no virtue today or any other day when it came to collecting fifty thousand big ones. *Oh, Lord, please, god, please let me get this money. I'll be so good. I won't strip no more, or have sex no more. I won't do nothing, I swear, god, please.*

Sure enough, thirty minutes later Daisy was walking out of the bank with a pocketbook full of wrapped, fresh, clean, one-hundred-dollar bills totaling $47,422. The four cents she slid into her jacket pocket. A bank manager had seated her in a private room and brought the money to her. She was allowed to count it. It turned out that the account had been frozen after the deposit was made. The bank had been informed by the government that the Social Security checks that Daisy had cashed had to be reimbursed because they should have never been cashed after Abigail Fothergill passed. Daisy had cashed three months' worth of checks, her mother's account was in the hole, and a freeze was placed on the account. Then, the bank had collected its debt, which was the $2,577.96 and therefore released the freeze, which allowed Daisy to withdraw the money out of the account.

"Take as long as you need, and if we can be of further assistance, just let us know," said the bank manager assisting Daisy.

"Thank you," said Daisy, staring at the cash. She didn't even hear the door close behind her. All she could do was sit there and look at the money. *Oh, my god, I can't believe it. Thank you, thank you, thank you.* It was as if someone else got blessed and she just happened to be standing next in line. *What am I going to do with all this money. I can live forever off of this. And the best part about it is, I don't have to sleep with nobody no more, ever!*

Daisy closed her pocketbook and got up from the table. She slid the chair back and closed the door behind her. She walked out of the bank and hailed a cab. She certainly had no intention of going down into the dark, creepy train station under the ground and being robbed by god knows who of her newly found fortune. *Uh uh, not me, no way.*

As she paid the cab and opened the door to get out, she saw Sticks watching her, standing only a few feet from the cab. Where he came from and how he got there, she didn't know.

Damn, it's only nine in the morning.

"Man, why the fuck you got me calling your phone like a fucking stalker?" he said, ready to grab her by her collar and throw her in some bushes.

"Sticks, I ain't even been home."

"Yeah, good answer. Come on, we got to go to the lawyer's office. I been trying to call you and tell you that the appointment is today at 10:30 A.M. Come on, you coming with me." Sticks began to walk down the street toward his parked car. Daisy wondered if she could outrun him. *Probably not.*

"Sticks, really, I don't want to do this. I'm not good at lying, and besides I don't even know this guy."

"You don't have to know him. Just memorize his picture."

"Yeah, but . . ."

"No, no fucking buts, do you understand," he said, his blood pressure at a boiling point. "Don't make me fucking hurt you,

Daisy, this is it," he said, gripping her by her jacket and really getting ready to knock the shit out of her.

Feeling his anger and knowing that she was no match for him, she decided to just play along. The only thing was the money. She wished she wasn't carrying it around in her pocketbook. Lord knows, anything could happen, and Daisy was a shining example of Murphy's Law; anything that could go wrong, would go wrong. An hour and a half later, Sticks walked them through the doors of the lawyer's office.

"Hey, Mr. DeSimone, this is Daisy. Daisy, this is Mr. DeSimone."

"Hi, Daisy. You can call me Bobby," he said, shaking her hand lightly.

Surprisingly, the lawyer wasn't that bad. He seemed to already know that she was a hired hand, and he didn't ask her a bunch of questions, but more or less told her what she would probably be asked and gave her all the answers to the questions. And after it was all over with, she wished she had talked to Mr. DeSimone before speaking with Detective Delgado and Detective Ross. Leaving the office, she actually felt better about the alibi. Bobby DeSimone, Esquire, had a way of talking as if he had it all mapped out and it was nothing but a piece of cake. He made her feel relaxed and told her everything would be okay. He handed her a subpoena on her way out the door of his office.

"See you guys in court," he said.

"All right, sir, see you Wednesday," said Sticks.

The only problem with the alibi was going to be Calvin Stringer, and unfortunately, she was the only one who knew that he would blow Sticks's alibi right out of the water in order to save his liquor license and the Honey Dipper. She thought about speaking to Sticks about what Calvin had told her, but decided not to. Truth was, she had no intention of giving that alibi, let alone even being in town next Wednesday.

Sticks turned onto Hadfield Avenue, pulled his car into a parking spot, and cut his ignition. He looked at Daisy for a moment, wondering what she was thinking. He had had a bad feeling about her, a bad feeling that she wouldn't come through, ever since last week when he tried paging her and calling her house and she didn't answer or return his calls. He knew then. He didn't dare speak, though; that would only bring heat on him. Daisy didn't understand the situation fully; it wasn't necessary for her. The only thing to do was to stick to the story. Nothing else mattered, at least not to Simon Shuller. As long as there was nothing that would or could end up leading back to him, no one needed to panic. But, the minute anything went down in the streets, a bar, a club, a train, a plane, wherever, and there was a remote chance it would bring heat back to him, he had no choice but to pick up the phone. And when he picked up the phone, oh, boy, it was a wrap. Reinforcements, silent soldiers, eliminators, and the cleanup squad would come through, and before Sticks could count to ten, Nard, Daisy Mae, and Sticks's black ass would become invisible, and poof . . . just vanish into thin air never to be seen or heard from again. Houdini couldn't do a better job. And the only reason he was still running around in the streets was that Simon Shuller was giving him the benefit of the doubt based on the fact that Nard was riding like a soldier, riding the time, riding for the murder trial, riding to win, riding to come home. That was the only reason Simon Shuller didn't blame his ass. He wasn't working the police, he wasn't snitching, and he wasn't cooperating. But had Nard spoken one word to the police or the DA's office, you best believe, the first weasel on Simon Shuller's eliminator list would have been Sticks, because it was Sticks who had brought Nard around and vouched for him. The second on his list would be Nard, and next up would be the last link to him, the chick who was giving the alibi, Daisy Mae Fothergill, or whoever the hell she was.

"So, we straight?" he asked, waiting for her to stick him for a couple of dollars. Everybody had some kind of story when it came to the almighty dollar. Sticks had heard eight million and one and counting.

"Yeah, I guess, Wednesday, right?"

"Yeah, Wednesday, you gonna be ready?"

"Mmm hmm," she said, looking away from him.

"Look, man, I ain't got time to be tracking you down, Daisy, man. Fuck that, I called you a hundred and one times, man. That shit ain't fucking cool, you playin' games, Daisy."

"Naw, naw, I'm not. I'll be ready. I just was running around, Sticks, you just don't know, times is hard, real hard. You got money, I don't. So, it's easy for you."

"Look, if you need a couple of dollars, Daisy, just let me know. What do you need?"

Daisy looked at Sticks as if he were from outer space. *Is this nigga serious? He ain't never been this kind to me, never. I have to haggle this nigga all night long to get five dollars, now it's whatever I need. Is he serious?* Daisy figured she would try her luck, see what happened.

"You know what I really need, Sticks?"

"What?" he asked, but thought to himself, *What the fuck do you want bitch, 'cause I think you playing games.*

"I need a car."

"A car," he responded. *Is she out of her mind? What the fuck I look like?*

"Look, you want me to testify for some nigga I don't even know. You want me to testify. Think about that, that's not what you said in the beginning. In the beginning you just wanted me to speak to some private investigator you said you hired. Shit, had I known that shit six months ago, I would have never said that bullshit to that investigator you had sitting all up in my kitchen. My momma told me not to do that shit too, but I didn't listen. Now, you got me all caught up in the middle of some shit, and I got to go to court and testify in front of a judge. Come on, for someone that I don't even know. I think that's worth more than a car, don't you?"

Sticks didn't know what to make of Daisy. First she was missing in action, not taking his calls. Now, she was speaking as if he owed her something, and technically he knew she had a strong point. He sat quietly looking out of the window, thinking how to deal with her. He didn't know if he should just punch her in the face, pummel her, and drag her into the courthouse, or if he should buy her a car and kiss her ass. He figured that, since court was in a couple of days, it probably would be better to do the latter and buy her a car and kiss her ass.

"You testify for me and I'll have a brand-new Jaguar waiting for you outside the courthouse. Whadda you think of that?" Sticks asked, having it all figured out.

"I think after I testify, you liable not to do nothing for me. I think you need to get my car before I testify. What you think about that?" she said, tilting her head to the side and puckering up her lips and licking them with her tongue at him, ever so seductively.

"A car, huh?"

"Yeah, Sticks, come on, please?" she begged as she moved closer to him, stroking his chest. "You know I take care of you, right? Don't I always look out for you? So, please, come on," she said, rubbing on his chest.

"Come here, come here," said Sticks, as he grabbed the back of her head with his right hand and with his left began unzipping his pants. He pulled out his dick, thick and fat, not quite rock hard, but definitely ready to seize the moment at hand, adjusted himself comfortably, and guided her head down.

Daisy obliged him, knowing that he would tip her, he always did, with a hundred-dollar bill. That was one of the problems she had dealing with Sticks's personality. Everything had to be done on his terms. If she took cash before sex services then she turned him into a trick, a john, or a business transaction. That would never happen. Sticks wasn't paying for no pussy. Even though she was a stripper, she had to fuck him for free, and that was that. It would kill his ego any other way.

Getting out of the car, she looked at him and asked again. "So, you gonna take care of that for me, before Wednesday?"

"I got you, I got you."

"Mmm hmm, right," she responded, knowing better, but it was okay, none of it mattered anyway. She was holding close to fifty thousand dollars in her bag and didn't need Sticks or nobody else at that very moment. *You ain't got to do nothing for me, Mr. Sticks, or whatever your real name is.* No, Daisy already had a plan and her plan was to get out of town, blow court, and take her fifty thousand dollars and start a new life, and she knew exactly where she was going to go: Murfreesboro, Tennessee, with her aunt Tildie and cousin Kimmie Sue.

PRICE OF LIFE

Daisy had a hundred and one things to do before Wednesday. *I only got one week.* She sat at her kitchen table sipping on a morning cup of coffee. *Should I pack and put my stuff in storage? I'll be coming back one day, maybe? Should I tell evil-ass Lester I'm breaking my lease? I don't know, I just don't know. If I go and get settled in Murfreesboro ain't no need to come back here, right?* She didn't know what to do about her apartment at all. That was a hard one. *Dr. Vistane got me scheduled for my abortion on Monday.* She began to look at Tuesday as her last day in the city. *I'll leave out Tuesday night.* Just then the phone rang. Daisy jumped up and answered it.

"Hello," she said into the phone receiver.

"Yo, Dais, the lawyer just called and said that they pushing the case back two more weeks. The prosecutors postponed it, okay. The new court date is the twenty-third, so be ready, you understand?"

"Yeah, no problem, I'm gonna mark it on my calendar right

now," she said, taking a pen and scribbling "court date" inside the twenty-third box on her calendar. She breathed a sigh of relief. *This is the best news I got all day. I got more time to disappear. Do I understand? Does he understand my black ass is getting out of Dodge? Let's see if you understand that!*

"So, what you doing?" he asked coyly.

"Nothing, just got up. Why, what you doing?"

"Nothing, I'm outside. I got something for you."

He hung up the phone, and Daisy looked at the receiver. *He got something for me?*

She quickly looked around her apartment. *I wonder what he got for me.* She picked up a pair of sweatpants that were lying in the corner of her bedroom. She put them on and slipped on a pair of slippers. Her hair was wrapped up in a scarf and she had on an oversized white T-shirt, complementing her baggy sweatpants. She grabbed her keys and headed out the door, making sure it locked behind her.

She walked outside and stood on the front porch. "Hey, Sticks, what's going on?"

"Nothing, just got something for you," said Sticks, holding up the keys to a Cadillac Seville. She just looked at him.

"You made me come downstairs for keys?" she asked.

He didn't say nothing, just picked up her hand and slapped the keys into it.

"What do I do with them?"

"I don't know, they for your car, so you can do with them whatever you want to," Sticks said as he motioned to a silver Cadillac parked across the street.

Daisy looked at him skeptically.

"What the fuck you looking at me all crazy for? Shit, that

muhfucker's right, right there. They don't make 'em like that no more."

"That's my car?"

"Yeah, you rolling now, baby. And she's clean."

"Wow it's beautiful. What kind is it?"

"It's a 1979 Cadillac Seville. It don't get more gangster than this, baby."

"Wow, I can't believe it. I can't believe you got me a car."

"Well, technically, I didn't get you no car. This here is from Nard. He's the one that got you a car. He wanted to thank you, for what you're doing. So, he got you a car."

"Wow," Daisy whispered to herself, unable to believe that she had the most beautiful shiny silver Cadillac in the whole world and it was all hers.

"He's taking care of the paperwork. By the time you testify, he'll have the title waiting for you," Sticks said, matter-of-fact. He had it all mapped out. Every detail was covered, and if it wasn't, it would be. Nard would come home. The entire case was circumstantial, even the girl who identified him from a photo in her hospital bed was dead. Who could be 100 percent sure to take her word on that? Anybody could build doubt around that. No, Nard would come home. It was just a matter of time. All they needed was one good witness to testify he was nowhere near the crime scene. Everything else was covered.

"Listen, Sticks, come here, sit down, please." They sat on the steps outside her apartment. "I can't take this car. I can't. It's too much."

"Yo, Dais, is you crazy, take the car. You saving a man's life, so go 'head."

"I can't save that man's life, Sticks. That alibi ain't no good, it's not gonna work."

Daisy wished in her heart of hearts that she hadn't said nothing, just took the keys and kept on going. She looked down, not wanting to face him.

"Man, listen, that alibi is good, Dais, we straight," said Sticks, confident and sure.

"No, it's not. Calvin said that guy, Nard, wasn't twenty-one and wasn't old enough to drink."

"What you mean, wasn't old enough to drink, and who the fuck is Calvin?"

"Calvin own the club. The police done been talking to him. They saying he wasn't twenty-one and can't be up in no bar. He said he wasn't losing his liquor license behind it and said he already told the police I wasn't working that night."

"Was you?"

"I think so, but shit, I don't remember."

Man, what the fuck? Just when one problem is solved, here go another fucking one. I thought that nigga was twenty-one, he stay in fucking neighborhood bars drinking. Fuck, why he didn't tell me?

"Who the fuck is Calvin?"

"Calvin, Calvin Stringer, the owner, my boss, hello . . . he done told the police I wasn't even there that night, he said I was off." She stopped and said nothing more. She didn't want Sticks to know that the police had paid her a visit too. *That should be enough. Maybe he'll figure out something else, so I don't have to testify now.* "He was so mean to me, he threw me out the club. I mean you don't know. I been messed up, I can't even tell you. Calvin wouldn't give me my job back and I haven't had no money, and nobody to help me."

Sticks asked her a few more questions about Calvin Stringer, like what he drove, where he would be at, what he looked like, how old he was, dark-skinned, light-skinned, and all the typical investigative questions. After being arrested and getting interrogated and having a long-term relationship with the police and detectives, a brother learns a few tricks on gathering information.

Daisy sat still and let Sticks think. He replayed what Daisy said one more time. He figured, from her telling him about Calvin, that she was to be trusted. He pulled out a thousand dollars and slid it to her.

"It's a grand."

"A thousand dollars, for what?"

"You said you lost your job, right? And Calvin wouldn't hire you back, right? Well that's to hold you down, okay."

"But, Sticks, the alibi, it's ruined."

"Don't worry about that. Let me handle Calvin Stringer. I got it all under control, you understand?" he asked, passing her the money.

"Yeah, I hear you," she said, taking the money, but knowing in her heart that there was no way possible that he'd want her to testify now.

"You sure you want me to take this money and the car, 'cause I feel bad?"

"Don't feel bad, shouldn't nothing be feeling bad about you, all that pussy you got, Dais," he said, and then he stood up, reached out his arm and helped pull her up as he felt between her legs. "I might come back over, check you out later."

"You better call first. I got a couple of dollars, so it's no telling where I might be," said Daisy, hoping he wasn't serious. She still missed Reggie—actually, she still had a glimmer of hope that he'd be back.

Sticks left, and Daisy watched his taillights until they faded. She walked down the sidewalk to where the Seville was parked. She sat in the driver's seat, placed her fingers around the steering wheel, and pretended she was driving. *Why does life have to be so complicated?* She was caught between a rock and a hard place. There was no doubt about that. Sticks still seemed adamant that everything would be okay, but deep down she had a bad feeling about the situation. *As long as I don't have to testify, I guess it will be all right. Sticks said don't worry about it, he said he'd fix it.*

She sat in the car a long time, thinking. She had her own problems to fix. She rubbed her belly. This would be the first thing. Deep down, she knew Reggie was the father, and she knew he wasn't coming back. She was hoping he would, even gave him a couple of extra weeks, but he had never showed up. She had waited long enough. Tomorrow was the big day, the big showdown. Dr. Vistane had her scheduled for Monday at 7:00 A.M. *At least I'm first thing, early in the morning.* She had strict instructions to follow. She wasn't allowed to eat or drink after midnight. She had to have someone pick her up and take her home. The doctor's office was not allowed to release her because of the anesthesia that would be used. She hadn't quite figured out who she'd call on, if anybody. But the last time she had an abortion, the clinic let her take a cab home, because she had lied and said her grandmother was at home waiting to take care of her. So, yellow taxi was starting to look like the designated driver. *God I swear this is the last abortion. I swear I won't get any more, ever.* She couldn't help but talk to herself. She couldn't help but to feel remorse about what had to be done. She honestly didn't mean to get pregnant. It just happened. *I wish I knew where Reggie was.* Then again, something told her that wherever Reggie was, he could just go ahead and stay there. *I know he's with another woman, he's got to be, to be gone this long. I can't believe he never came back, just never came back.*

DR. VISTANE

Daisy arrived at the abortion clinic on Thirty-eighth and Haverford Avenue at 7:07 A.M. She was on time and ready to go. A receptionist was behind the desk. She watched as Daisy walked through the door and approached her desk. She already knew why the young girl was there.

"Who are you scheduled with today?" she politely asked, pulling Dr. Vistane's booklet after Daisy answered her. She took Daisy's name, checked it off in the log, and handed Daisy a clipboard with forms attached to it that needed to be filled out and some information—pamphlets on abortion, what to expect, and other information, such as side effects and recovery. Daisy took the clipboard and had a seat in front of a floor-model television that was turned to the early morning news. Daisy listened to the reporter read off the wave of current news events. She finished her paperwork and handed the clipboard back to the receptionist.

"Okay, just have a seat and the nurse will be with you shortly."

At seven-thirty Daisy was led up a flight of stairs and into a small nurse's office where she had her temperature taken and her blood pressure checked and then was handed a small cup to go to the bathroom in.

Daisy answered all the nurses' questions, used the bathroom, and then sat in the waiting area until she was called into the procedure room, where she undressed, put on a robe, and lay on a table. Minutes later, a doctor stepped into the room. It was the anesthesiologist, along with her gynecologist, Dr. Vistane. Dr. Vistane lifted her legs and placed her feet in the stirrups at the ends of the table as he asked her several questions, double-checked that she hadn't eaten or drunk anything past midnight, and then began to explain the procedure and everything that would be happening. Daisy sat there listening to the anesthesiologist first and then Dr. Vistane. Truth was, she had heard it all before. Actually, it seemed like yesterday, and she remembered it all. *Let's just get this over with,* she thought, thinking of the last time she was there.

"Wait, I thought I was just getting a needle, local anesthesia like the last time?" questioned Daisy.

"No, Daisy, we're going to put you to sleep. Don't worry, it's better this way, you won't feel a thing," said Dr. Vistane, smiling down on her.

"Just begin to count backward from one hundred," said the anesthesiologist as Daisy began to count, not making it to ninety-two. Daisy's head was heavy, and she felt amazingly free, the highest of any high she had been legally administered, and it felt great. Before she knew it, she was asleep.

Dr. Vistane performed anywhere from four to eighteen abortions every day at the clinic. The patients were mostly black, as the clinic was located in an all black neighborhood. Dr. Vistane was in his mid-forties and had a family of his own at home. Even though abortions were frowned upon, Dr. Vistane felt he was actually saving poor, black souls. Dr. Vistane believed that blacks were the lower class, not just financially, but all the way around the board, and to help rid the world of another black bastard baby was something that needed to be done. *Just look at how they live, and the men don't provide, the homes are broken, the children lost, and their neighborhoods are all crime-ridden.* Yes, he was doing great humanitarian work.

It wouldn't be until late in the afternoon that Daisy would come to, her head aching, her body sore, her abdomen cramping.

"Hi, I'm Stephanie, and if you need anything just let me know."

Daisy's head was spinning and she waited a few seconds as she watched the room stand still.

"Here, take this, you'll probably have some cramping," said Stephanie, placing a heating pad on her stomach.

"What time is it? I feel like I've been sleeping all day."

"You have, it's four-thirty."

Four-thirty? What in the world did he do to me? I been asleep way too long. Maybe they just gave me too much anesthesia.

"I'm really hungry and thirsty."

"Okay, wait, I'll be right back." Stephanie quickly went behind the nurses' station and into a back room. She came back out with a small paper cup of ginger ale and a packet of crackers.

"This is only two crackers," said Daisy, trying to remember the last time she ate.

"No, eat that and drink that first and if you don't get sick, I'll give you some more. Just try to rest right now. I'll be back to check on you. Here, I'll turn the television volume up for you," said Stephanie, as she stood on a chair and raised the sound from the television.

"Thank you," said Daisy.

She lay in the chair and closed her eyes. The abortion was over, whatever had been growing inside her was gone now. It was a relief. Sad but true, Daisy could barely take care of herself, let alone another human being. The television faded in the background until she heard a news reporter. "I'm standing outside the Honey Dipper where a brutal murder occurred early this morning. It appears that Calvin Stringer was closing his strip club for the night when a witness claims that he saw two men wearing masks and carrying guns enter the establishment and within seconds he heard gunfire erupting, leaving fifty-three-year-old Calvin Stringer dead. Police have no suspects and have no motive at this time."

Behind the news reporter you could see two EMT workers pushing a gurney with a black body bag containing Calvin Stringer's body. He was taken across the parking lot, the gurney folded down and lifted into an ambulance.

"Oh, my god, oh, my god," whispered Daisy. A sudden nervousness fell on her shoulders like a heavy magnet and stuck to her. She thought about the night before. How she told Sticks what Calvin had said, how he threatened to testify that she wasn't working that night.

"The alibi isn't going to work."

"Don't worry about Calvin Stringer, I'll take care of him."

Sticks's voice echoed through her as she looked at the television. *What if Sticks killed him? Sticks killed Calvin for the alibi.*

She remembered the last time she saw Calvin alive. She had tried to get her job back at the Honey Pot.

"Please Calvin, please. I need my job, I need it."

She didn't have to tell him that. He already knew it. But Daisy had gotten herself caught up with some real bad people and Calvin didn't want no part of her escapade.

"Get on out of here," she heard his voice bellow as he closed his door in her face. That was the last time she saw him.

Daisy turned her head and wiped her eyes. She was certain that it was because of her that Calvin was dead. "Oh, Calvin, I'm so, so, sorry," she whispered as a tear rolled down her face.

The taxicab dropped Daisy off in front of her house. She looked across the street at the Cadillac Sticks had bought for her. A part of her wished that she had never accepted the car. *That's okay, I'm gonna use that car to get the hell out of here. That's what I'm gonna do.*

She went into her apartment and began to pack up all her and Abigail's personal belongings. Everything she planned on taking with her, she began to lay out neatly on the bed. *I ain't never coming back here. In my heart, I already know I ain't coming back to this place.* She had a few pieces of living room furniture, a small table and four chairs in the kitchen, and her mother's bed and dresser. Not much, but enough that she didn't want to walk away from nothing. *What am I going to do with this stuff? Don't really matter, because where I'm going, I won't need it.* She hated to part with her mother's things and her mother's clothing. Just having Abigail's clothes still hanging in the closet was a comfort to Daisy, making her feel that she wasn't alone, even when she was. She went over to the closet, reached up to a top shelf and took down a red shoe box that she had been using to hold her prize winnings from the bank. She looked in the box. It was all there. All the money was in place, just as she had left it. She sat on the bed and fumbled her fingers through the paper bills. The anesthesia was wearing off and she was feeling tired, her head was beginning to ache, and her abdomen was sore. She lay down, holding the box of money by her side as she drifted off to sleep.

Bang, bang, bang!

Daisy jumped from a peaceful sleep. She sat up and listened to the sound of someone banging on her door.

Bang, bang, bang!

"I know you in there. Come on out here. Don't act like you don't know it's me. You know who it is, Daisy."

Is that evil-ass Lester? A month done went by that fast? Damn, let me get up. Daisy put her feet on the floor as she heard Lester at her door again.

Bang, bang, bang!

"Okay, I'm coming, Lester, chill out, you gonna break the damn door," she said as she unlocked the bolt, cracked the door, and peered out at him.

"What the fuck you peeking at me for, looking like yesterday. Don't peek at me, open the damn door," Lester Giles demanded. "That's the problem now, it's my god damn door, don't nobody got my money on time in this motherfucker and I'm sick and tired of it. Just sick and tired of it. You getting out of here, you hear me Daisy? You got to go."

"You want me to leave you the furniture?"

"I don't care what you do, but you gon— What you just say?"

"I said . . ." she paused for a moment, getting control of the conversation. "Do you want me to leave the furniture?"

Lester stood silent, not saying anything.

"Look, Lester, it's just not working for me no more since Momma died, and I'm leaving, I'm getting out of here. I'm going back down South with my aunt Tildie and my cousin."

"You mean them family of yours that visited for the funeral?"

"Yeah, my aunt and my cousin. I'm going to stay with them now."

Lester looked around the apartment and decided the furnishings weren't that bad. *Shit looks all right, pretty clean looking.*

"When you leaving?"

"I don't know, Lester. I'm getting my things together, now. But, I um . . . just taking step by step, right now." She shook her head, not really knowing if she was coming or going.

"I don't owe you rent, 'cause you was just here and I gave you some pussy and the month ain't even went by. What, you back for more?"

Lester grew silent. He was thinking. First of all he had someone willing to pay him double the rent she was paying. Not to mention, he was holding three months' security deposit from Abigail. *Daisy probably don't know that,* he figured, so why mention it. "Well . . . um . . . no, I guess if you're moving on, and you leaving the furnishings," he added, lifting his eyebrow and staring her down for an answer.

"No, I'm not taking the furniture, just my things, my clothes, you know."

"Well, then, I'll clear your tab. You know you owe me about two months' rent. But, I like you, Daisy, I'm gonna let you slide."

"I thought we took care of my tab the last time you was banging on my door like you were crazy. Come to think of it, Lester, as much pussy I done had to give you to live in this rat hole, you'd think that you owed me something by now."

Lester stood calm and still. He thought silently. "Shit, you probably is right," he said, breaking into laughter. Daisy didn't find his humor entertaining at all, and she just watched him as he laughed so hard, he couldn't catch his breath.

"Look at your face," he said as he laughed at her some more. "I can't take it. I got to go, I got shit to do."

You need to have something to do, Lester Giles, landlord from hell. She watched him walk down the hall and take the staircase up to the next floor. *He's probably going to harass someone else for their rent money or even worse.* She thought of all the times she had entertained Lester Giles, giving him sexual favors in exchange for the roof over her head. *I wonder who else Lester Giles got sexual favors from in the building.* Little did she know, he got favors from every woman he could in exchange for rent. It was his little dirty secret and always had been. His wife didn't have a clue, but sure enough, Lester Giles purposely took young, single female tenants in hopes that they would fall on hard times, find themselves between jobs or at a loss, and need desperately to keep a roof over their heads. *Thank god, the bank made a bank error and gave me all that money,* she thought to herself. *I woulda had to sleep with Lester again next month.*

No sooner had she closed the door than the phone rang. *Why aren't people still asleep?* She walked over to the phone and answered it on the third ring.

"Hello."

"Didn't I tell you, let me handle things, and look what happens, now we straight," said Sticks, talking in circles but actually hitting the bull's-eye on point.

"What you talking 'bout, Sticks?" she said, unable to keep up with his fast talk and half conversation.

"Your man, Calvin Stringer. Shit, you can go on over to the Honey Dipper and get your old job back if you want," he added.

Is he out of his mind?

"So, Dais of the week, is we straight? How you like the car?"

He's insane.

"It's all right, I haven't had a chance to drive it yet."

"Why not?"

"I been sick, Sticks. I feel better today, though."

"All right, well check this. I got to go, I got to get out of here. I'll call you back and don't forget, we on like popcorn for the twenty-third."

Daisy couldn't believe him. He had as good as admitted to killing Calvin. Not directly, but indirectly. Daisy hung up the phone and began moving around the apartment. She was okay from yesterday and she was ready to go, ready to get away while she had the chance. *I can't believe he killed Calvin. He's crazy, he's really crazy. What if he does something to me? He wouldn't do nothing to me, would he? Damn, this shit is getting way too heavy.*

Daisy packed up everything she would be taking and even packed up some of her mother's deepest treasures to give to her aunt Tildie. She had eight large trash bags and five medium-sized boxes of everything she owned in her life. *I ain't got no choice. I stay here I'll probably end up like Calvin, or worse, incarcerated for perjury like the police said. I ain't got no choice, Sticks ain't leaving me none.*

She had made up her mind and she was ready to go. There was nothing left for her in Philadelphia but bad memories and a series of murders, sex, drugs, and a bunch of gangsters. *I got to get my life together. I just got to.* Daisy had never ever imagined getting herself in this much trouble. She had never thought that her associations would or could lead her down the scariest, deadliest path in her life. *Why did he kill Calvin?* It was as if he could have killed anybody else and it wouldn't have mattered that much to her. But she knew Calvin, she had worked for the man for over a year. There were times when he was mean as a pitbull, barking and biting at the girls. But, in his own way, he was simply Calvin, a man. And like any other man with an ounce of character and integrity, he took care of his girls and he took care of his business. He was respected for that among his peers and even in the community, considering his profession.

Daisy sat holding the phone in her hand. She looked at the dial pad. For some reason, she had done everything she needed to do but call her aunt Tildie and cousin Kimmie Sue.

"Hello, praise the Lord," said Tildie answering the phone.

"Hello, Aunt Tildie, it's me, Daisy Mae."

"Daisy Mae, oh, Daisy Mae, my, my, my, isn't it just something special to hear your voice. Honey, how you been, darlin'?" said her aunt in the deepest country accent you would ever hear a person speaking. Every single word she spoke was whispered with a southern twang.

"Well, I don't know, Aunt Tildie. I just been really going

through it," said Daisy as she began to break down crying. She was crying for her mother, whom she missed terribly. She was crying for Reggie, because he had pretended he loved her, she was crying for Calvin Stringer, because he was dead all because of her. She was crying because she was scared, scared of the mess she had gotten into.

"Oh, Daisy Mae, don't cry, sugar. It's gonna be all right, you just got to have faith in the Lord, honey. You just got to believe and put your trust in him."

You just don't know, Auntie Tildie, you just don't know.

"I was wondering if you think I could come down there and stay with you and Cousin Kimmie for a while, 'cause I just really want to be around family, Aunt Tildie, and you're the closest memory I got to my mom."

"Oh, Daisy Mae, come on down, honey. You don't have to ask, we'll take care of you, don't you worry. When do you think you might be coming to visit?"

Daisy wasn't expecting the question because she was caught off guard by the word "visit." *Who said anything about a visit?*

"Well, actually, I was thinking about leaving tomorrow and riding down there."

"Tomorrow, my, my, my, that's mighty soon, oh my," said Aunt Tildie, now the one caught off guard. "Um, you don't give much notice, do you?" she asked, then quickly added, "Well, don't worry about it, you just bring yourself on, and be careful out there."

Tildie gave Daisy Mae the basic directions that would get her into the town of Murfreesboro. She'd be okay once she got into Nashville and picked up TN-840.

"Call us from the road, and let us know how you're making out, okay? We'll be waiting on ya to get here."

"I will, Aunt Tildie, I will," said Daisy Mae before she hung up the phone. *I wonder what she's gonna say when I get there with all these bags and boxes of stuff. She don't know, I'm not just visiting. Maybe I should have told her, probably would have been nicer if she knew I planned on coming to live there. It'll be okay, that's what family's for.*

First thing come daylight she'd hit the road. Her destination, Murfreesboro, Tennessee. *I'm ready. I'm ready to start a new life and leave this old one behind.*

ON THE ROAD AGAIN

Interstate 76 West led her out of the city and onto I-81 South. That was the bulk of her highway time, close to five hundred traveling miles across the green countryside. Interstate 81 passed through Maryland, West Virginia, Virginia, and from there she crossed the state line right into Tennessee. It took her a day and a half to reach Tennessee, but she finally made it. She pulled over to the side of the road and at rest stops so many times to rest and catch sleep that she had lost a lot of time. Daisy couldn't imagine being a trucker. *How do they drive those big rigs up and down the highways without falling asleep?* She had made several calls, letting her cousin know she was okay. Kimmie Sue had given her driving instructions from off I-640, which would put her on Broad Street close to where her aunt's home was.

Five hours later she stood outside a gas station waiting for her cousin to arrive.

"Girl, I'll be right there to getcha, you can just follow me right on home," said Cousin Kimmie Sue, twang dripping off every syllable.

Kimmie Sue pulled up in a black 1979 Ford pickup truck. She was waving and smiling from ear to ear. Elated to see her cousin, she jumped out of the truck and hugged Daisy, spinning her around.

"I am just so excited to see you! I always wanted you to come and visit. I did, I truly did."

"Well, here I am. Even though I'm really not quite sure where here is. There's no lights nowhere," she said, as if Kimmie Sue could turn some on.

"This the back of the woods, girl. Murfreesboro is out there. But you got Nashville, well, at least the town of Nashville, and there's lights there," she said convincingly.

"Well, how do we get there?" asked Daisy jokingly.

"Oh, it's easy, Murfreesboro Road leads you right into Nashville. I'll take you into the city, don't you worry. Come on, let's get out the dark and get on in the house," said Kimmie Sue.

Get out the dark, that's an understatement. Daisy peered out at the vast darkness behind the one and only, lonely gas station with no real name. It was desolate. *How did Momma grow up down here?* Part of the reason she chose to come to Murfreesboro was her mother's being born there, living there half her life, and having the only family in the world there. *I don't know, though, I don't even see no buses or trains or nothing.* Coming from Philadelphia, a thriving metropolis with mass transit, buses, trolleys, and lights at night, one could move around. But Murfreesboro, it was a tad slower . . . seemingly still. The sound of distant crickets, which heightened while driving with the window down, could be heard in the near distance. Even with the window up, she could still hear the crickets. And not one car, no people, no traffic, no red lights, no nothing; it was scary in the wide open dark country, to say the least. What if something happened? And the roads had no sides, just a yard of dirt, some grass that led into a never-ending ditch and then, simply put, farmland . . . miles and miles and miles of farmland. Getting stuck out there, broken down, or god forbid anything else, was something she didn't even want to imagine.

"Shh, I don't want to wake Momma up," said Kimmie Sue. "Come on, follow me," she said, leading Daisy into the house, past the living room, down a hall to a doorway and staircase that led downstairs into the basement.

Kimmie Sue was twenty-two years old. She was five feet seven inches tall and weighed only 135. She was a very pretty girl, just as striking as Daisy was to the eye. The girls, side by side, could pass for sisters, in fact. Kimmie Sue and Daisy Mae both had the same length and grade of hair, but Kimmie Sue had small brown eyes, and bushier, fuller eyebrows than Daisy Mae. Kimmie Sue's hair was sandy brown, and the hot Tennessee sun was beginning to turn it sandy blond.

"You hungry, Daisy Mae? You want something to eat?" asked Kimmie Sue, ready to sneak her a sandwich or some chips from the kitchen.

"No, I'm okay. I'm just tired a little, ready to lay back."

Kimmie Sue got a pillow and a blanket out of a closet for Daisy. She turned on the television, made sure that Daisy Mae was comfortable, then curled up on a love seat next to the sofa. The two girls talked and talked until the wee hours of the morning, falling asleep only hours before it was time to wake up.

"Hey there, Daisy Mae," said Aunt Tildie, as she stood above

Daisy, waking her out of her sleep. "Girl, look at you. Ain't this something?" she asked, as Daisy opened her eyes. "How was your drive down?"

"Good," said Daisy, smiling at her aunt.

"Well, get on up, we best be heading out to church. Sunday services, Kimmie Sue, so let's get moving. I got some biscuits, sausage, eggs, rice, and gravy upstairs if you want some." She walked over to the love seat. "Hey, do you hear me, Kimmie Sue? I'm talking to you, come on, we got to get a move on, I'm fixing to get on out of here. Let's go!" She smacked Kimmie Sue across her bottom.

"Ma, come on, it's too early," said Kimmie Sue.

"Kimmie Sue, if I've told you once, I've told you twice, the Lord is always on time, so we must be too. Besides, the early bird catches the worm, right, Daisy Mae?"

I'm not trying to catch no worms. I'm trying to catch up on my sleep. But she opened her eyes and sat up as she watched her aunt moving around the basement room picking up from the night before.

"You hungry, come on and eat, before services."

Services, what services is she talking about? "What services, Aunt Tildie?"

"Church, we go to church every Sunday and every Wednesday night for Bible study. I'm sure you will enjoy yourself praising the Lord with us at the Trinity Spirit Worship House of God."

Daisy almost choked.

"Goodness, you okay, honey?" she asked as Daisy absorbed her twang and the hold she had on words, stretching them out as she talked. She shook her head that she was fine as the word "church" rang through her ears, dissected itself, and punched her brain as if Sonny Liston himself had delivered the blow.

"Oh, and you want me to go?" she said, already knowing that she wasn't doing nobody's church, not today, not tomorrow, not happening.

"Of course," Tildie demanded. "Of course, I do. Besides, it just wouldn't be right to leave you and not make sure you were included in the glorious praising of our Lord," said Tildie as she ascended the stairs.

"Yes, it would be," mumbled Daisy to herself. *I ain't never been inside a church, outside a church, or nowhere near a church. Oh, damn, damn, damn. Let me get up. Did she say something about Wednesday nights? She'll probably take us to church Thursday too, while she's at it. Thursday night is ladies' night at the clubs, or at least it is in Philly, how am I gonna be up in somebody's church and at the club.*

"It'll be okay. I met my boyfriend, Dusty Mitchell, at the Trinity Spirit Worship House of God. Trust me, you'll like it. Maybe you'll meet some people there. Dusty will be there, he's in the church choir. He's real smart too," said Kimmie Sue, nodding with every word she spoke. "Oh, I'm so glad you're here. I can't wait to show you off to everyone at the church. This is going to be so great, right," asked Kimmie Sue, filled with confidence.

"Yeah, I guess it will be," she said, smiling at her cousin. "I guess it will be," she said in a lower tone to herself. *Oh, no, she wants to show me off. What am I going to do?*

She followed Aunt Tildie upstairs to the kitchen. Aunt Tildie had it all laid out on the counter. Some sausage, biscuits and gravy, rice, and some scrambled eggs.

"Go on, help yourself and hurry on and get dressed." Aunt

Tildie didn't really remind her much of her mother; they were two completely different types of women. Aunt Tildie was the country mouse and her mother was the city mouse. Aunt Tildie was very, very neat. Abigail cleaned up after a mess, maybe the next day or the next. Aunt Tildie made the beds, old school with the hospital corners, made all the meals, did the cleaning, and stayed on top of Kimmie Sue like a hawk. Even though she was only a couple of years younger than her sister, she was better preserved and much healthier, getting around on her own with ease, still capable of driving, whereas Abigail needed help just standing. The two sisters had lived completely separate and different lives, and Abigail's life had been a little harder, less fortunate, and less financially secure than Tildie's.

Tildie had eaten and bathed, then made breakfast. She went to her room to get dressed.

"So, where's there to go."

"Oh, nowhere much, where do you want to go?"

"They got clubs down here?"

"Yeah, they do. They got night clubs and party spots. But Momma would probably die. Oh, my, Daisy Mae, you go out in the big city and all?"

"Yeah, don't you?" said Daisy. *The club, shit, my ass is the damn party. The club, hell yeah!*

"Shhh, don't talk so loud. Momma says them kinds of places is filled with whoremongers and heathens and the Lord did not intend for our bodies to gyrate against one another unless a union amongst souls has been blessed, so I don't know how to dance. Shhh, don't tell nobody," said Kimmie Sue matter-of-factly.

She's serious, is she . . . either that or she's crazy. What have I got myself into now? If it ain't one thing, dammit, it's another.

"Wow, you've never been to a club, and I've never been to church. Isn't that something?"

"No, it's not something, it's pretty bad if you really think about it. How have you never been to church? Aren't you saved?"

"I don't know," said Daisy Mae, shaking her head, not having a clue and not even sure what "being saved" entailed.

"Shhh, don't let Momma hear you saying that," warned Kimmie Sue as Tildie came around the corner.

"What you was saying, don't let me hear you saying what?" she asked, seeming stern and tall even though she was only five-four. "And why ain't you dressed, Kimmie Sue? Come on, girls, I don't want to be late."

"Okay, Momma, I'm getting dressed now," said Kimmie Sue.

"I'm not sure what to wear," said Daisy as she thought of how she spent most of her Sundays resting up. That night life of dancing, stripping, and rubbing on men sure did tire her out by the week's end. She didn't have a formal dress, just a few hooker-looking shoes for dancing up and down on her pole and some jeans and T-shirts. Not one pair of dress pants. Maybe she had a few dresses in her bags and boxes, but they were party dresses, short, revealing, way too sexy, nothing she could possibly wear after looking at her Aunt Tildie's Amish motif, very plain, simple, nonrevealing, and gray. *Damn, what in the world is going on down here? What is Aunt Tildie fucking wearing?*

Sad but true, Daisy Mae had jumped right out the pan and into the fire. She had realized Aunt Tildie was religious when they came up for her mother's services, but so much was going on that Daisy didn't really pay attention. Her mind had been elsewhere.

"I, um, didn't realize I would be needing my church clothes. I wasn't thinking."

Aunt Tildie dressed Daisy Mae as best she could, fitting her in one of Kimmie Sue's church dresses and giving her a pair of flip-flops for her feet. "God ain't looking at your feet. He's looking at your heart. Come on, now, let's mosey on, we're running late. Kimmie Sue, let's go."

Daisy realized that her aunt and cousin were faith fanatics, and she had driven herself into the middle of nothing but farmland. She wasn't sure if she had made the right choice or a horrible mistake coming there. So far, the odds were leaning toward "horrible mistake."

CATCH ME IF YOU CAN

Three Weeks Later

Vivian Lang cut through the parking lot of the Federal Bureau of Investigation and entered the downstairs lobby. As she stepped into the elevator and pressed the number ten, Nathan Chambers suddenly appeared and smoothly held up his hand, opening the elevator doors.

"Good morning, Agent Lang."

"Good morning, Agent Chambers." She smiled, holding her hands tightly behind her back, dress suit perfectly starched, legs perfectly straight, and pumps holding up her frame like a Barbie doll.

"I have a surprise for you today," he said, smiling.

"Really?" she said, smiling at him with her baby blue eyes as she tossed her blond hair around. "You, Agent Chambers, having time for surprises? Please hold back no more and do tell."

"Ah ha, you are right," he said as the elevator stopped at the tenth floor and the doors opened. "I do not have time for surprises." He spoke sternly, cleared his throat, and as if in another world, completely changed his demeanor as he stepped off the elevator.

"I received a call on your case, another tape sent over last night. It should be on your desk. Take a look. Hey, Bob."

"Hey, Mackenrow," added Lang, walking through the hall-way while considering every word her partner said.

"Okay, so back to where I was, it's a real person this time, and she withdrew fifty thousand off a bad check put in the account months ago."

"You're sure she's real, no phony ID," asked Agent Lang, un-able to believe they finally had a break.

"It's the biggest break in this case. This is the thing though, listen to this, the bank claims this girl, and I can't remember her name, oh fuck . . . some flower, anyway, she was cashing the Social Security checks of her dead mother."

"Who deposited the check?" asked Agent Lang.

"That's just it. The bank claims the mother made the de-posit, go figure, and she's dead already, according to the govern-ment. Geez, who fucking knows, these people are really sickos," said Chambers, wondering what type of person would use her dead mother to cash in on. He couldn't help but comment. "Then again, it's probably the dead mother's ghost making the deposit."

"You're probably right; it wouldn't be the worst case I've seen," said Lang.

Agent Vivian Lang couldn't wait to get to her desk. She im-mediately grabbed the package, opened it, and looked at the tape. It had three segments listed by date. She put the tape in, sat on the corner of her desk, with the remote control in her hand, and pressed play. It was a little old woman, walking into the bank with a male escort—a black woman, elderly, gray hair, hunched, old-looking dress and sweater, glasses, walking with a younger man, wearing jeans, sneaks, and a long-sleeved, button-down shirt. They walked over to the teller and handed her the deposit slip and the check, a few seconds passed, the deposit slip record was returned, and the two were walking away and out of the bank.

Next scene was the same little old lady walking into the bank alone, walking over to the teller line, waiting in line, giving the teller a check to cash, conversation. Teller left the window. Agent Lang pressed pause on the remote and picked up the file folder on her desk and looked at it. The folder and outline from the bank showed that the account had been frozen. The bank stated the teller did not have information about why the account was frozen, and after relaying information to the old lady, who presented herself as Abigail Fothergill, according to the records, the teller claims that the customer left the bank immediately and did not return. She pressed play, watched the teller return and the old lady leave the bank. Agent Lang looked closely, as the old lady seemingly was walking faster as she left. She pressed rewind and watched how slowly the woman was moving as she walked in. She pressed forward and watched how fast she was walking out. Vivian Lang continued to read the bank statements as she peered up and looked at Daisy Mae Fothergill, "receiver of funds," as the bank had titled her.

"Oh, my God, what in the world? Look at what this girl is wearing," said Agent Vivian Lang to herself as she watched a scantily clad, high-heel wearing Daisy Mae with mile-long legs and short shorts enter the bank and make her way over to the teller window.

Agent Vivian Lang watched as it appeared that Daisy and the teller began to argue and the teller pointed her over to customer service. There she signed in, a woman approached her, took her to a desk, spoke with her, left, came back, left, came back and escorted Daisy over to a private booth. Daisy counted her money, put it in her pocketbook, and walked out of the bank.

What was wrong with this picture? Why did the bank give her the money?

Agent Lang began to read the folder: looked like a bank error. The freeze was dropped by this woman who had no record anywhere of why the freeze was there, so the bank technically had no reason to freeze the account anymore. The phony check cleared, they were repaid for the Social Security checks they had cashed, so everyone was happy. The bank customer service representative had no reason not to unblock the account.

Who is Daisy Mae Fothergill, the "receiver of funds"? What's her angle on all this? Way too many pieces to this puzzle and still no arrests.

Agent Lang popped the tape out of the player. She needed to enhance everything on the tapes so she could see more about the suspects. She needed head shots and she needed to do a major background profile on Daisy Mae Fothergill. If she conducted a proper investigation, by the time she had Ms. Fothergill indicted, she'd have all the pieces of the puzzle fitting in their places. That's how the Federal Bureau of Investigation operated. You weren't indicted if they weren't sure or were trying to build a case or if the bureau had nothing better to do with you. Oh, no, if you were indicted by the FBI it was because you were going to prison and the case had already been built and all pieces of the puzzle were already present. That's just how it goes, federally speaking.

Sticks was sick, so sick he could vomit. His stomach ached and twisted from anxiety. He hadn't slept or eaten in days. The stress was building, and day after day he tried to reach Daisy. He went to her apartment, night after night, pounding at the door and waiting outside for a sign someone was home. No lights. He called and called, no answer. For the past four weeks, he had been chasing Daisy like a mad stalker. But to those around him, he remained cool, calm, and collected, well balanced and in control. He was only pretending—deep down, he was sweating bullets. He played it off, though, to Nard, convincing him he had nothing to worry about.

"Naw, you good. I got this, let me handle it. Once this broad testifies, you outta there. You hear me, outta there. Don't worry, baby boy, you'll be home in a hot flash," he said with feigned confidence. Nard believed him too. He had put all his trust and faith in Sticks. That trust and faith was what got him through the days and nights of utter confinement. It wasn't until he walked into the courtroom the day his trial was set to begin that he began to worry. He surveyed the rows of benches filled with scattered faces until his eyes met Sticks's. Maybe it was the look of "I'm sorry" or maybe it was the way he shook his head to the left and bent his gaze to the floor, but at that moment, Nard knew the witness with his alibi wasn't coming through, and for the first time he was scared. He knew deep down in his heart that there was no way he could give the system life, not his life, maybe somebody else's but, Lord, please, not his.

Nard took a seat next to his counsel. The room had a soft chatter as Bobby DeSimone took time to brief his client.

"Listen, the witness isn't here, and honestly, I'm nervous. She's our entire case, you understand, Bernard. We need her testimony."

"Sticks said she'd be here."

"Yeah, well, looks like Sticks is wrong. She's not here. My office has been calling her, Sticks told me he went to her house every day, morning, noon, and night, looking for her and called her a hundred times. She never answered the door, never answered the phone, and honestly, I think she's gone. I could be wrong, but I think she's gone."

"Gone? Gone where? She's got to testify or I'm going to go to jail for the rest of my life," said Nard not wanting to believe his probable fate.

"Listen, Bernard, we're gonna handle it. We got to see how all this plays out. I might be able to get a plea deal. I can talk to the DA and we can plea this thing right out if this girl doesn't show. For today, though, we need to get a continuance."

Tommy Delgado swung open the double wooden courtroom doors and walked into the courtroom, over behind the prosecutor's desk, shook prosecutor Barry Zone's hand, whispered in his ear, and peered over at the defendant and his lawyer.

The prosecutor was betting his last dollar that DeSimone would request a continuance, and sure enough, DeSimone approached the side of his wooden table.

"Hi, Bobby DeSimone," said Bobby extending his hand.

"Barry Zone," responded the DA, grasping DeSimone's hand, returning the hello.

"Listen, I'm in the position of having to request a continuance, based on my witness being out of town. I'm not comfortable with going forward."

I bet you're not, thought Delgado to himself. He thought of the one time he had met the alibi witness. She was unknowing, scared, and had the most intriguing shade of green eyes he had ever seen.

"Yeah, sure, why not? I won't object, it's the judge's call," responded Zone, looking over at Delgado to see his reaction.

Sticks sat patiently still, silently praying that Daisy would walk through the door. Of course, he knew that she might or might not have gotten the gist of the situation and how critical her testimony was, not only for Nard, but for him, and the predicament her failure to testify would create. He got up and walked out into the hall. He dialed Daisy's number and listened as the voice operator said the number had been disconnected. *Disconnected? This bitch done disconnected the damn phone? What the fuck. She knew we had court on the twenty-third. She knew that shit.* The day had come and gone and he sat and watched as his man stood in front of the judge with no witness and no alibi. DeSimone did the right thing. He immediately asked for a continuance, not wanting to move forward with the trial. The judge granted the postponement. The court date was scheduled for two months away, on the third of October. The judge banged his gavel and court was adjourned.

Simon Shuller paced the floor of his small office in the back of Fabulous Willie Man's barber shop off Twenty-seventh and Susquehanna. He had been popping Tums and antacids all day, with no relief. It was no surprise that Simon Shuller's health was failing. He was getting too old for the stress of it all, the worry and frustration of the streets and everything that came with them. Not to mention the black man wasn't black no more. Or at least that's how he felt. Simon Shuller was an older hustler, and truth was he was beginning to frown upon the young gangsters of today. Back in the day, the streets had codes and real men upheld and honored those codes. Not the young, hip, gangster types you saw on the streets today. Simon Shuller was more of a quiet man, not too flashy, but styled and classy. He ran the streets with an iron fist and was in on everything. Simon Shuller was the man, in charge of everything from drugs to numbers. Yes, he was the one who ran the numbers game for Philadelphia. Every night you had the Lotto and you had the street numbers. If you won, it was Simon Shuller who paid out, but for the most part, Simon Shuller won and paid nothing. Night after night after night that money went into his pocket right where it belonged—at least to hear him say it, it did.

"Man, that pacing you doing is making me dizzy over here," said Dizzy, one of the few people Simon Shuller trusted to a degree. Dizzy James had been his friend for over forty years.

"Well, good then . . . Shit can match your name," said Simon as he stopped, said his few words, then went back to walking the floor. "I should have handled this shit from the beginning. I should have followed my heart."

"So, what's the investigator you hired sayin' now?"

"Lasworth ain't said nothing but what I already know."

"What's that?"

"They fucked up. The alibi for the kid was a no-show. And Sticks, the motherfucker's a walking nightmare. Instead of him coming to me, you now got a string of murders following behind the Somerset Killer and it's just a big mess," he huffed, shaking his head, picking up his medicine bottle, and popping a few more pills.

"That god damn medicine gonna kill you."

"Shit, I'd be dead without it," he joked back, hating that time was truly the grim reaper, but sharing the laugh with his old comrade. "But, naw, Dizzy, man, the mole say this kid Nard is a real thoroughbred, a trouper. He's not talking and he's gonna ride, even if it means the worst. He wants his family taken care of, especially his mother to be looked after, you know? But that fucking Sticks got that kid jammed up. He wasn't where he should have been and now he gets the kid jammed up with no alibi and shit, 'cause no one can find this girl."

"It was Sticks who set this kid up with the alibi?" Dizzy asked. He had heard little about the story up until now.

"Yeah, and if he didn't pay the girl, it would explain why she didn't show up for court," said Simon as he stood back up, exhaled, then sat back down.

"You all right?"

"Naw, I'm not," said Simon, looking at his oldtime friend. "Ay yie yie, you know the only thing is, if the girl was paid fifty thousand dollars, why she wasn't there?"

"What did he say? Didn't you ask him?"

"Of course I asked him. I'm telling you, this guy is not fucking thinking with his head on straight. He's not covering the bases. His story to me was that she had a death in the family and had to leave town, that she would be ready the next court date. I don't know, just don't sound right, for fifty thousand, you don't need to be at no funeral, motherfucker already dead. Shit, she was supposed to be there."

"You right, Simon. When you're right you right. She should

have been there and nine chances out of ten, you're right about this Sticks character. He's no good. I'll put a call into Mira, he'll be able to track this girl down. If she's still breathing, he's your guy, he'll find her, no matter where she's fucking hiding. And Sticks, I wouldn't keep playing around with him."

"If I find out he took that money and didn't pay the girl, Daisy or whatever her name is, I'll bury him with a stick in his ass. Fucking stupid-ass kid, what the fuck is this guy thinking?"

"I don't know what these guys out here today even got going through their minds. But I'll find you a stick and have it on hold, 'cause something's telling me you gonna need it," Dizzy said, hoping some comedy would ease the tension. He had known Simon for a long time, and in his heart of hearts he knew that if Simon found out this guy Sticks was up to something, he would bury him, stick in his ass and all.

Sticks pulled out of the parking lot and replayed his conversation with Simon Shuller in his head. It didn't sound like anything was a problem. Simon took the postponement news and moved on to another matter. That eased Sticks's mind automatically. But deep down inside, he knew Daisy had to be found, and that was his number-one priority. She really was the straw that broke the camel's back with her disappearance. *She knew we had court. She knew we was supposed to be there. Why the fuck did I give this bitch my old car? Fuck, something told me not to.* He pulled up on the block, but didn't see the Seville. *Man, where is this chick done disappeared to?*

"Fuck!" Sticks commented as he hopped out of his car and quickly made his way up to Daisy's building. He began ringing her bell and banging on the front door, so loud that Lester heard the commotion inside Ms. Selda's apartment on the third floor.

"Hey, hey, what's all the noise about?" said Lester, after making his way down the stairs, as he opened the door to the building of the apartment row home.

"I'm looking for Daisy."

"Daisy's gone; she don't live here no more," said Lester trying to slam the door on the thug standing before him.

"Gone, where she go?" questioned Sticks, quickly using his foot to prevent the door from slamming. He pushed the door back hard and busted into the vestibule of the row home. "Who the fuck is you?" he asked, lifting Lester up off the ground and onto the wall. "How the fuck you know she gone?" he questioned, choking Lester half to death.

"I'm . . . I'm . . . the landlord. I just know she . . . gone, that's all."

"Where she go?" asked Sticks.

"I don't know," said Lester, and it was at that moment that Lester decided to take a stand. He was tired of the young thugs running wild in his neighborhood. Young men and boys, as young as twelve years old, trying to be gangsters and thugs, carrying guns, intimidating the community, and running around believing that they was so bad and determined to run something. Lester wasn't having it; you wasn't running Lester Giles.

"Let's see if this can help you remember," said Sticks, pulling out a gun and pointing the barrel at Lester's forehead, his finger on the trigger.

"You think that gun makes you a man, son?" Lester asked him, coming from the old school and hoping he could talk some sense into the young man standing before him.

"Nigga, shut the fuck up, don't ask me no fucking questions." Quickly, he took the tip of the gun and whacked Lester in the head. Lester took the blow, falling back against the wall and down to the floor as blood began to run down the side of his face. He held his hands over his head and face, fearing that Sticks would hit him again. "I swear to God, I'll kill you in this motherfucker. Get the fuck up the stairs and let me in this bitch's apartment," Sticks ordered, grabbing Lester and forcing him up the staircase.

"Yo, old man, you need to start talking, for real. I know she left a forwarding address with you, I know she told you something. She wouldn't have just left."

Lester tried to lie. "She didn't tell me nothing. She just left, that's why all her furniture is still here."

The apartment had been cleaned. Sticks began searching, looking for a forwarding address. But Daisy had been pretty clean about leaving, knowing that she was leaving her apartment to Lester. All her personal stuff she had taken with her, and everything else, she had bagged up and left behind for trash.

"Listen, I know you know something. You can tell, it's all over your face. I know she told you something." Sticks began to roughhouse Lester, pointing the gun at his head, threatening to pull the trigger, punching him with uppercuts and jabs. Because the man was old, Sticks had the advantage.

"You know what, I'm not even gonna play with you no more. I tell you what, if you don't tell me something, I'm going to kill you right here and now, motherfucker, so this is your last fucking chance," said Sticks as he spun around, getting madder and madder at Lester. "Do you hear me?" Sticks screamed at him. "This is it, tell me where she is before the count of three."

He put his gun to the old man's head and counted one. Sweat was pouring down the sides of Lester Giles's face and he saw his life flash before his eyes. He heard Sticks count two. He knew he was going to die on three.

"Wait, I know where she's at. She's down in Tennessee, down in Nashville somewhere where her peoples live at. She's got an aunt, I don't remember her name. That's where she told me she was going," he said, shaking his head yes, for certainty.

"Why the fuck didn't you just say that shit? Why put me through all this shit? Stupid fucking old-ass man," said Sticks as he lifted his foot and pounded it down on Lester, kicking his side, cracking his rib.

"Aaarrr, help me, Jesus. Please, mister, please stop," said Lester, unable to take any more pain. "I've told you all I know," he said before collapsing.

"You should've told me sooner," Sticks said as he raised his gun and brought it down on Lester Giles's head again, leaving Lester Giles lying on the floor.

Sticks kicked him again and turned and walked away, not realizing that the beating he had given the man had caused a stroke. Lester Giles lay on the floor struggling for his last breath. Blood gushed throughout his brain cavity. He was already paralyzed by the time Sticks drove down the street and turned the corner, and in twenty-two more minutes he would die lying on the floor of Daisy's apartment.

SECRET AGENTS

Agent Vivian Lang and Agent Nathan Chambers were ready to speak to Daisy Mae Fothergill. They had pulled her last known mailing address and checked every bureau database, collecting a profile on her. They had everything from a prior arrest for soliciting a police officer to cashing her mother's Social Security checks after her mother was dead. Yes, they had her entire history. It all popped up on the screen in black and green. Vivian could see where she even had a subpoena issued in a state court proceeding. And Agent Vivian Lang had every intention of following up on that lead and seeing where it led her.

Ms. Selda from the third floor was on her way downstairs just in the nick of time. Just as Agent Lang was about to ring the door bell, the door flew wide open.

"Excuse me," she said, recognizing them as the police, undercover officers like those on her show, *Law and Order. Mmm, I wonder who's in trouble, probably that girl on the second floor, she looks like a bunch of trouble. Maybe it's that damn Lester, they could take him on to jail right now for me before rent comes due next month.*

Nathan walked in first, looking up the stairs. He took his gun out of his holster on the side of his suit jacket as Agent Lang did the same. She carefully closed the door behind her, making sure it locked. They went up the stairs and knocked at Daisy's apartment door. No answer. Agent Chambers twisted the knob, and the door opened with a creaking sound as Vivian Lang pushed it as far open as it would go.

Agent Chambers, gun in hand, moved silently to the right covering the dark and unknown territory as he moved into the apartment and down the hallway toward the bedrooms, keeping his back against the wall, his eyes piercing the empty apartment. Vivian Lang made her way to the right of the door and peeked into the kitchen. It was clean. She moved to the end of the wall and peeked around the corner.

"Chambers, I got a body," Lang called out, surveying the room and confirming that it was clean. Chambers finished his search of the bedroom, turned around, and followed his partner's voice into the living room.

"Okay, I am so not here right now. Don't touch it!" he ordered with stern conviction.

"How long you think he's been here?" she asked, knowing that Chambers was forensics' key guy.

"Looks like days. Come on, get away from it. All you need is a fiber or a hair to fall on this guy."

"Damn, we'll make an anonymous 911 call."

"Yeah, sounds great," he said, wiping the doorknob with a handerkerchief. "Don't touch anything. Fuck, I hate finding dead people."

"Boo, Chambers," she said, tickling his side. She pulled out a pair of gloves from inside her skirt suit jacket, put them on, and begin sifting through the apartment, her gun still in hand and ready.

"There's nothing here. She's gone. You think she's using an alias?"

"Why would we be so fortunate?"

"Hey, we've seen stranger, come on, let's get out of here before someone else sees us. Fuck, man, I see fucking Grayson from Internal Affairs. I fucking see him with a big light and you know what, he's flashing it inside my asshole."

"Oh, Chambers, give it a rest, will you," Vivian spat. "Where is your heart, man?" she asked, as she fumbled through a kitchen drawer. "Look, Aunt Tildie's phone number. What good, loving niece wouldn't keep in some kind of touch with Aunt Tildie," said Vivian, waving a piece of paper. "Isn't six, one, five Tennessee?"

"Fuck me! Oh, geez, why do I have to get stuck with the partner from 'I'm-just-looking-land,' with a dead man on the floor.' I'm bent the fuck over. See me now. I see it, I see it now, all for Aunt Tildie's phone number."

"Hey, it beats a blank, this could be the lead we need to catch this girl. Stop whining, come on, let's go."

"No, from now on we follow the rules."

"What fun would that be?"

The next morning the police followed up on an anonymous tip, called through the 911 line, along with a missing persons report the police finally let Lester's wife, Euretha Giles, put on record.

"So, where do you think she is?" asked Merva, biting into a hot dog, standing outside Daisy Mae Fothergill's building as the body of Lester Giles was being brought out on a stretcher.

"I don't know, but wherever she is, she's got some pretty ugly people looking for her."

"Yeah, pretty ugly isn't the word. Everybody around this girl is coming up dead. Calvin Stringer, her boss, now her landlord, I mean come on, that poor girl and her son, and for what? And you were so nice to her, caught up in cleavage I guess," she said, changing her tone, trying to be funny.

"Um, Merva, for the record I was not caught up in cleavage and I, unlike you, was giving her the benefit of the doubt. I still am. You can't blame these deaths on her. She didn't pull the trigger, or beat anyone to death. She's running, and she's scared."

"She's a prostitute, a stripper, she'll do anything for money, anything. Do you think she cares about these people? Why are you constantly passing out validity to these people?"

"What's these people, Merva? The less fortunate, to some degree, look at the way of life, I mean, come on."

"No, you're right, so everyone gets a pass for crime then? Huh, because they're impoverished, or just financially inept, or life's been so hard, they can't get right so they can just commit crime in your book."

"Come on, Bernard Guess is the one on trial, not Daisy. So, if I was nice, if I'm understanding, then so be it. I don't think it's her fault and she should be held accountable. Now, if she testifies against state, I will be the first to put the cuffs on her and throw her in a cell and make sure she don't see the fucking sun shine. But, right now, she's not our problem."

"She's not the first. What about the black kid, what was his name, robbing corner stores with a BB gun."

"Maxwell Brittingham," answered Tommy, remembering the black kid he had let go two times for trying to rob a corner store with a BB gun.

"Exactly, and you remember their names, go figure!" she said, scratching her head, looking at him, trying to figure his psyche and having yet to come close. "Have you ever thought that there's something off with these people? And this girl; trouble. Jesus, Tommy, if there's one more death surrounding this scrawny alley cat, I'm going to scream."

"Listen, Merva, they've named her as a witness, not us. I tried and I offered state assistance, police protection, the whole nine. She ran, point-blank. So, if she does end up dead, that's not our fault."

"How are you using the word 'our'?"

"Listen. After the body of Calvin Stringer was found . . . we fucked up, we should have had our hands on her, but she was gone, and by the looks of it, she packed, Merva, she moved her stuff out, and she cleaned the place out, leaving nothing but furniture. Merva, they have to produce her, not us. Technically, we don't need her at all in the courtroom, they do. Hey, I hope she runs and keeps running. I hope she hides and they don't find her."

"She's lucky, she better keep running, if she know what I know, 'cause these guys are tracking her down, and when they get her, she's gonna be lucky if she don't end up dead somewhere."

"Listen, they got thirty days to locate their witness. After that, it's a wrap and Bernard Guess, he's toast. And you, you need to not worry about who I want to save. You might need me to save you one day."

"Whatever," she said.

"Come on, this crime scene is a wrap," he said as the team leader of forensics waved his hand, letting them know they were done with the investigation. Lester Giles had taken a bad blow to the head and suffered a stroke. His cold body was stiff and bloated as the coroner gently rolled a dead Lester Giles over face up, onto a thick, black, plastic bag and then zipped it up.

The next day, the captain had their asses in a sling.

"We got another murder that links back to this Somerset Killer case. Another murder?"

"Captain Dan, all we know so far is that Lester Giles went to answer the door and never returned to the third floor to fix Ms. Selda Crest's toilet. She thought he got caught up in something else and would come back. He never did. The wife put out a missing persons report. And the police received a 911 call about a dead man in the building."

"Yes, sir, while he had a stroke, he was also beaten in the head badly. We're waiting for the coroner's report, which should be in today. So, we'll know the exact cause of death."

"I want this murderer brought down. I want this witness found, because she knows something and I want to know what she knows."

"I agree with you, Captain." Merva smiled at her partner. "Don't you agree the girl needs to be brought down too, Delgado?" asked Merva, really smiling.

"Yeah, I agree," said Delgado, waiting to wring her neck once the captain was through.

"There's a meeting in an hour. The Somerset Killer might be in jail, but he's got a cohort or cohorts and they are still out in the streets. We have to bring these people to justice. I want you to track this girl, Daisy Mae Fothergill, wherever she is. Hunt her down. Trust me—with this string of bodies that's being left behind, it's all leading back to this one girl. You find her, you'll save the next victim."

NEW LEAVES

The chase had begun, and everyone was searching for the same thing, Daisy Mae Fothergill, like a cat chasing a mouse, but this little mouse had many cats following her trail. But Daisy was transforming her life and trying to get a job. She had gotten her résumé together with the help of Kimmie Sue, and she had been faxing it out every day over and over again to the various job positions in the newspaper. She remembered the day her aunt came to her looking as if the sky was falling.

"Um, Daisy, how long are you planning on staying here, because I just looked in the back of your car and you really got a lot of stuff in there."

"Yeah, I do, Aunt Tildie, I sure do. I brought it just in case I decided to stay here."

"So, you're not going back?"

"No, I don't think so," said Daisy Mae, blinking at her aunt, shaking her head no. "Nope I'm not. But, don't worry, Aunt Tildie, I been looking for an apartment and going to this office supply store every day faxing out my résumé. I think I've found a place out on Murfreesboro Road heading toward the city. And I got a call back for a job interview in a doctor's office. Isn't that something. So, I'll probably get my apartment, Aunt Tildie, this weekend, and I'll need some furniture, but I'll be all right."

Aunt Tildie was speechless. "I hope you get your place and a good job. I'll pray for you, Daisy Mae, that those things come. I'll pray to the Lord," she said, moving in on Daisy, placing her arms around her, and hugging her tightly. "God bless you, honey," she said.

Daisy had been staying with her aunt and her cousin for about a month now and it was time for her to move on. Tildie was glad she'd be close by, and she was glad that Kimmie Sue had her cousin, someone in the family in her life besides herself. Daisy Mae was content in Nashville, more so than out in the sticks of Murfreesboro. At least Nashville had some lights at night for her to look at. There was always something about the city streetlights that captivated her. She thought back to her old life and how she had been living, and the way she had earned her living. She thought of Felix and wondered where he was. *Eeeww, let him stay there. Don't even think about it.* She quickly erased the memory. And then she looked around at where she was. A calmer place, where the city moved just a little slower and the people waved and wished one another a smiling "howdy," short for "how do you do," and no one was in a rush, no one seemingly had anywhere to be. Was it possible that no one cared about time, or that time didn't hold as much importance as did the moment? And for her, it seemed that all the smiling faces washed away the bad ones, that time was healing her and time had taken her to another place, somewhere far away, where there was the possibility of reinventing herself. She felt bad for Calvin and prayed for his soul every day. She still had not heard about the murder of Lester Giles, in her very own living room, again all because of her and her alibi.

Sometimes, out of sight really is out of mind, and her past life and the people she once knew were out of mind and nowhere in sight. She liked it like that, wanted it to stay that way. She was in a new place, with collages of new people to meet, greet, and get acquainted with. She was where she wanted to be, and it was easy to block out the old memories of the yesteryears. It was easy to forget her turmoil-ridden past, and it was easy to let old dogs lie down and rest. She was an old dog wanting to lie down and rest. And at only twenty-two years of age, she had ripped and run the streets and everything in between them, she was ready for a change, ready for a fresh start. She had lived and experienced enough life-altering chances and changes; she was "old beyond her years," as the old folks used to say, and truly a blessed woman to still be alive. She was starting to feel as if God had something in store for her, something grand and unimaginable in store for her life. She definitely knew she had been given a fresh new start and she was ready to take it.

Just then the phone rang, and Aunt Tildie picked it up.

"Hello." She paused. "Yes, son, hold on," she said, smiling at Daisy. "It's Billy from church calling on you. Here you go," she said, passing the phone to Daisy.

"Hey, Billy, uh huh, sure, the movies, sure thing, hold on. Kimmie Sue, want to go to the movies with Billy and Dusty?"

"Do I? You got to ask? I'm going bored out of my mind. Momma? I want to go."

"Yeah, Aunt Tildie, we should be home before it gets dark, okay?"

"I don't see why not; those are fine boys, come from good homes. I know their families well. I'll help you girls get ready," she said, hoping for a proposal for one of them. Where Tildie came from, life was so much simpler. You fall in love, you get married, you have babies, raise them, and then live out the rest of your life, together, of course. Now there really wasn't much more to life than that.

Daisy had met Billy at the church. He was a nice, decent, well-mannered, gentle young man. He had a factory job, working for an ice-cream manufacturer. He ran the conveyor belt that put the lids on the tops of huge ice-cream barrels. If he did that the rest of his life, it was just fine and dandy by him. He was content with lids. He found another fulfillment in his life with his church, as did most of the members. And he loved sports, all kinds of sports. He was an attractive man, with distinguished features. He dressed very casually in khakis and button-down shirts and simple loafers. He was used to pretty girlfriends and talking on the phone to women whom his friends would die for the chance to say hello to, but he had an animal attraction that was magnified by his smile. Daisy couldn't take her eyes off him. From the first time she saw him, she melted, just looking into his eyes.

"How are you today?" he asked politely.

"I am really fine, now," she said, smiling like a young schoolgirl.

"You sure are. You're not from here, are you?"

"No, I guess you can tell, right?"

"Pretty much . . . Yeah, you don't sound like you're from these parts."

"No, I'm not."

And from that simple conversation budded a new courtship within the Trinity Spirit Holy Worship Church. All the elders gossipped, excited at the talk of a fresh new romance. It was as if spring was in the air in the middle of fall.

"Well, don't they make a fine couple?" they'd ask each other.

Pastor Maykims heard of the new courtship, and one Sunday after church called them into his office.

"Now, Daisy Mae and Billy, it has come to my attention that the two of you have fallen smitten with one another, is this so?"

The two of them, startled and completely caught off guard, looked strangely at one another, not sure of each other's response. They had only been courting for two weeks.

"Um . . . well . . . I do . . . I mean, I think that, well . . ."

"Yes, Pastor we do . . . like each other," she said, smiling at Billy, letting him know she could speak for them.

"Well, young lady and young man, no fornicating, there can be no fornicating in the Trinity Spirit Holy Worship Church. Sex is for marriage. This is what the Bible teaches, and it is for you to do your job, young lady, your job, and do you know what that is?" asked Pastor Maykims as he frowned and bent his head, looking over the top of his glasses into her eyes.

"Um . . . well . . . I do . . . I mean, I think that . . ." she said, sounding like Billy looking for relief, but finding none in his silence. "The answer is that the Bible teaches us not to fornicate and not to do that," she said, hoping that her answer was correct.

"Yes, very good, Daisy Mae, but it's more than that. You are a woman, like Eve was to Adam, and you must place your modesty in the hands of the Lord. Do you understand, young lady?"

"Yes, Pastor Maykims."

"Well then say 'Amen.'"

"Amen," said Daisy and Billy in unison.

Daisy had never seen anything like it. *You'd think people would have something better to do.* Had she known it would be put on display, a bullhorn introduction into her personal business, she would never have gone outside with the boy. The fact that Billy Bob Porter liked her and was courting her around town was the biggest news flash of everybody's life. *For Pete's sake, I wish I had known all this would be going on.* But the cat was out of the bag, as they say, and there was nothing she could do about it.

The next morning, Daisy got a call from the Shalat Apartment Homes. She was approved for a one-bedroom, one-bathroom apartment, and as soon as she hung up the phone, she got two more calls, regarding her résumé. She had sent it out via fax after looking through the newspapers at the Help Wanted section. A law firm in the heart of Nashville was looking for a receptionist, no experience required, minimum wage, just answering phones. The other place that called her back was a telemarketing firm.

The first thing Daisy did was get dressed, hop in her car, and make her way down to the leasing office for her new apartment. The leasing agent had a package of forms for her to fill out and a set of keys. Daisy had her security deposit and first month's rent. She counted the money out on the table and smiled at the leasing agent before handing her the cash.

"Now, you know we do take checks for you to pay your rent, if that's more convenient," the woman said, looking at all the crisp bills fresh from the mint.

"Here you go, don't forget your welcome pack," the leasing agent said, smiling from ear to ear. Daisy couldn't take the keys out of the woman's hands fast enough.

Daisy opened the door to her apartment. She walked in and looked around at the empty space. She closed her eyes and pictured each room, and how she planned on decorating. Nothing fancy; simple and plain would suffice. She had never had her own place before. She had always lived with her mother. She looked at the set of keys in her hand. *The Lord sure does work in mysterious ways,* she said to herself, thinking of the old folks and counting the number of times she had heard the saying before. Daisy pictured a sofa and a table and a recliner filling the space in the living room. A table and some chairs for the dining area with a lovely centerpiece, fresh-cut flowers and some hanging curtains in the windows would complement the empty space. *I can't believe I got my own place. Momma, can you believe this?* she asked her mother, as if Abigail were standing beside her. So much was happening for Daisy. She had job interviews scattered throughout her calendar for the upcoming weeks. *I know I'm going to get a job. I can feel it. Please God, help me find a job. I sure could be a telemarketer and I'd be really good too. I like to talk and sit and dial phone numbers. And, God, I could definitely be a receptionist, greeting callers over the phone, sitting at a desk being professional.* It was at that very moment she thought of being Carol Burnett and passing a call into Mr. Wiggins. *No, seriously, God, I can do it, I can. Please, God, please let me just find a job.* Daisy had been caught in the rapture of the hood, the essence of the ghetto, and the urban decay of the inner-city streets for so long that the possibility of being a receptionist was like a dream come true to her. And being an ordinary receptionist was just as good as being a brain surgeon, or at least for her it was. *I sure do hope that I get a job. Maybe I should pray. Pastor Maykims did say to just call upon the Lord and ring his phone. He will answer day or night.* Daisy stood still for a minute, and then in the middle of her apartment, she bent her knees, dropped down, and, positioned comfortably on the floor, she prayed.

TRAINING DAY

The next morning Daisy walked through the front doors of the law firm, introduced herself to the receptionist, and was taken into a side office. Daisy Mae sat in front of a desk, an empty chair beside her.

"Ms. Murtaugh will be with you in one moment," the small-framed white girl said before closing the door, bobbing her ponytail behind her as she made her way down the hallway.

Daisy Mae looked around the tiny office. Plaques graced the wall, pictures graced a desk, and a border of file folders sat on the floor next to all open wall space. *I want a desk so I can decorate it too,* she thought to herself, picturing her own workspace.

"Hi, Ms. Fothergill," said a tall woman with blue eyes and long blond hair, wearing a business skirt suit, high heels, cleavage, and no pantyhose. *Look at her,* Daisy thought to herself.

"Yes, thank you for letting me interview with you today," said Daisy, standing up, holding out her hand.

"Oh, please, sit down, relax," said Debbie Murtaugh,

shaking the young black girl's hand. "Would you like something to drink?"

"Um, no, I'm fine."

"You sure? No water, soda, nothing?" said Debbie, before closing the offer.

"No, I'm okay."

"So, let's take a look at what we have here," said Debbie as she moved some folders around, stacked them neatly on her desk, opened another folder, and looked at Daisy Mae's résumé.

"And what is the Honey Pot?" she asked.

"It's a restaurant; I was a host. I would greet the guests and sit them at their table and if they needed something I would get it for them." She admonished herself to pretend to be her cousin Kimmie Sue. Every word she spoke was just as Kimmie Sue had taught her to speak after countless hours and days of rehearsals. She was ready for her first job interview, on the outside. But on the inside, she had a real bad case of the jitters.

"Did you ever do any sort of phone work?"

"Well, I would have to answer the phones from time to time and make dinner reservations. I'm very comfortable with talking on the phone, I do it almost every day," said Daisy, smiling at Ms. Murtaugh.

"Yes, dear, don't we all," said Debbie trying to figure if the young black girl in front of her was sharp enough to answer the phones and take messages. It sounded easy, but it could be overwhelming.

"Where did you go to school?" asked Debbie.

"I graduated from Overbrook High in Philadelphia. That's where I'm from."

"I see that. So you recently moved to Tennessee."

"Yes, ma'am, I have family down here and my mother recently died. So I came down here to be with family."

"Oh, I see," said Debbie. "Well, let me tell you about the firm and what we do here."

Daisy sat and listened as Debbie Murtaugh explained the firm, the partners, and the exact job description for what Daisy would be expected to do. At minimum wage, it was a no-brainer. Answer the phones, direct the calls, take messages. *She looks like she can handle that. She is very pretty. The partners might not like the fact that she's black. They'll get over it. Damn, look at the time, I have to meet Chuck Daly at Cristo's. Shit, I won't have time to get my nails done. Dan wants to go to dinner tonight. What will I wear, my little black dress . . . that always works. Let me wrap her up and get her out of here, I got less than twenty minutes to get to Cristo's. What the hell is she over there talking about? I haven't heard one word the poor girl's said.* Debbie sat across the desk, shaking and nodding her head, a smile, but no teeth, and a slight frown on her brow.

"I know that if I get the chance, I would be a good reception-ist for your law firm."

"I'm sorry, what did you say?" asked Debbie Murtaugh.

"I said I just need a chance, but if you hire me, I'll be the best receptionist you ever had. I really want this job," Daisy said, her green eyes piercing Debbie's baby blues.

"Can you start tomorrow?" asked Debbie.

Daisy couldn't believe the words she had just heard. *Can I start tomorrow? Is she nuts, does she have to ask? Of course I can start tomorrow.* She could start right now if Ms. Murtaugh needed her to.

"Yes, ma'am, I sure could. I could start right now, if you want me to," said Daisy jokingly.

"No, I have lunch right now, but tomorrow will be fine. Be here at 8:30 A.M. and be ready," said Debbie Murtaugh, eyeing the young black girl as she slipped into a pair of tan leather Manolo Blahniks under her desk and stood up to lead Daisy to the door.

"Thank you so much, thank you, really. I'll see you tomorrow . . . eight-thirty . . . sharp."

"Yes, thank you, see you tomorrow," said Debbie, extending a soft and gentle hand. She took Daisy's hand into hers and looked at Daisy as she closed her office door. She walked over to her maple desk, picked up a note pad and crossed off one of the several tasks on her "to do" list. *Now, the offices have a receptionist, the partners can stop complaining, and I have lunch with Chuck.*

Daisy Mae was so happy she didn't know who she would tell her simply marvelous news to first, but she couldn't wait to tell somebody. She just wanted to scream out to the world how great she felt. *Can you believe it? Can you actually believe it? I got a real job. Wait till I tell Aunt Tildie and Kimmie Sue this.*

She was more confident than ever that Tennessee was the place for her. For the first time in her life, she felt like she had a vision, a plan, a path for her life. Somewhere out there was her destiny, she just had to take care of herself long enough to find it. Sometimes, Daisy would go out to Beaver Dam Pond down the road from where her aunt Tildie lived and look out at the water, thinking of the past and all the demons she had escaped. At the right time of the day, the pond would glisten like a shadow of gold as the sun quietly nestled itself between the vast forest of trees, its rays of light shining from above, just a blink away from sundown. And Daisy would sit on the same large rock where she always sat, looking out at the calm, tranquil pond, and she'd talk to God. It was her way of asking God to forgive her for all she had done, all she had been a part of, and all she wished she could change. And it was there she drew strength. It was there, in what some would call "the middle of nowhere," that Daisy found the most majestic spot on earth, and it was there that she found faith and knew that God was beside her. *I won't never do nothing against you, father God. Please just let me have a good life, enriched and full of happiness, and a life full of love.* That was always what she would ask God for, and honestly, she was changed. Daisy would starve on the street before she would sell her body away. No, not her, not no more. She'd never be sacrificed that way ever again, a naked, lost soul on display for men to lust after, pay, have their way with, then walk away from, still a man. She had always felt this was less than she deserved. But it was a combination of things that had Daisy twisted out in the streets of Philadelphia. Her momma had tried to talk to her when she was alive. The last person who wanted to see Daisy stripping and living that kind of life was Abigail. She never judged her baby, just tried to ask her questions and say things to her, so that maybe one day she'd change. Little did Daisy know, the spirit of her mother was right there with her, sitting next to her, like a whisper in the wind.

I got so much to do with myself, so much to do. And she did. She had her new job and was making the commitment to be the best receptionist ever. God knows, stripping ain't easy. But it was easier than working for crazy white folks all day. Daisy realized that being a simple receptionist wouldn't be as easy as she had thought it would be. The corporate world was complex, and so were the people in it, especially the white people, and the truth was she hadn't really captured the art of functioning in both worlds. Now the hood, she had that down to a science, but working in the law firm, that was a whole new ballgame. And somehow, some way, Daisy had managed to get herself on first base. *I'll be okay, I can do this. I can take care of myself now.* That's what she told herself the next morning as she rode into town for her first day at work.

"Good morning, Daisy, let me take you around, show you the offices and everyone here."

"Good morning, Ms. Murtaugh."

"Call me Debbie, please. Ms. Murtaugh would be my mother. So, where are you from? Your accent isn't quite country," said Debbie, tossing her blond curly hair as she walked Daisy down a hall and pointed at offices, introducing her to the various partners and associates who worked at the firm. No one looked for more than a split second and those on the phone didn't even do that, just stayed focused on the task at hand as Debbie and Daisy peeked into offices and around doors.

"That's Victor Hatland, he's the senior partner of the firm. Lose his calls, lose your job. Always take messages, always get phone numbers, and a good receptionist must know the three threes," she said as if the fate of the universe depended solely on her ability to take a message.

"What's the three threes?" asked Daisy, completely and totally clueless.

"The three threes are who, where, and what. Who are you? Where are you calling from? And what is your call regarding?"

"Ohhh," said Daisy.

"Exactly. Don't forget it either. And whatever you do, never patch a telemarketer or a sales call through to the partners or their secretaries. All those calls come to me, you understand, so make sure you screen everyone until you're more familiar. Jack Delany takes all his personal calls personally. Do not send them to his secretary; if he's not in, voicemail. Got it?"

"Yes, ma'am."

"If there's ever a call and you're not sure what to do, just take a message. Eventually, you'll get the knack of it, after you're more familiar with the partners and everyone here. All the partners have one secretary, and they share paralegals. There's what we call the 'team chart' in your employee hand guide. You need to study that team chart. It will really help you become familiar with names and people."

"I will, I'll memorize every name by heart."

After making a walk-through of the offices, with brief introductions to partners, secretaries, paralegals, and law clerks, they were back at the front desk.

"Just remember you are the intro to the firm. Be professional, sound professional, speak clearly, and be courteous to our clients. Other than that, it's really a no-brainer."

Honestly it wasn't. Daisy just knew she could do the job. However, her first day, she almost flunked out. The phone lines were ringing off the hook. David Sternberger's secretary had to help Daisy answer the calls.

Debbie's solution was that each secretary would take an hour out of the day to help cover phones and assist until Daisy got caught up.

If she doesn't get the hang of it after a week, she's outta here. There would be no ifs, ands, or buts about it. Debbie would never sacrifice her job as office manager for any of the employees she hired for the firm. But, after a week's time, Daisy did get the hang of things: All calls were answered by the third ring and the calls were promptly handled and precisely directed through the small switchboard, which Daisy had lied and said she was familiar with, but honestly didn't have a clue about until the other secretaries helped her master it. No, Daisy was doing really well at her new job. She was always on time, getting up a half hour early just so she wouldn't be late. She always dressed professionally, wearing pumps, skirts, and suit jackets. Her style sense was noted by the other secretaries and paralegals. She even made a friend, Jack Delany's secretary, Mary Martin. She was a white girl with blue eyes and long blond hair, but she had grown up in a predominantly black neighborhood.

"Oh, we got a litte bit of this and a little bit of that in my neighborhood, we just all live together like one big happy family," she said, looking like Dolly Parton, just not as heavy up top, but then again, no one is that heavy up top. But it was her smile that invited you in. Friendly, pretty, and just happy, with the biggest smile, outlined by red Cover Girl lipstick and shined up with a layer of lip gloss on top. Mary Martin's smile would light up a room like a Christmas tree.

"Hey, Daisy Mae, you want to come with us? We're going to Jerry's Pool Hall a little later on tonight, get a few drinks, mingle with the menfolk, and just have a good ol' time. Me and some of the girls here always get together on Friday nights and do a little partying. You wanna come along?"

"Aww, wow, thanks, Mary, but Billy's picking me up after work. He wants to take me home to have dinner with his parents."

"Well, ain't that something. Are you excited?"

"Am I? I met them before at the church, but just said hi and bye. Oh, my God, now I have to sit at a table with them. I've been sitting here all day just as nervous as nervous can be. Look, look at what I've done to my nails, I'm just sitting here biting 'em off. I'm so scared. What if they don't like me, what if his momma don't like me?" said Daisy, fearful of the possibilities.

"How is she not, look at you. Stop worrying, it'll be fine." Mary Martin bent and gave Daisy Mae a quick hug. "Have fun," she said, waving bye-bye.

Dizzy opened the wooden door with one hand, holding his towel around his potbellied waist with the other. The heat from the sauna hit him as he stepped inside and closed the door behind him. The lights were off and the room was silent, still. With his towel wrapped around his waist, he sat next to Simon.

"What's going on, slim?" Simon Shuller joked as they both laughed.

"They found the girl. She's working in a law firm down in Nashville, Tennessee."

"Nashville, Tennessee? What the fuck is she doing down there?"

"They say she got family down there. This kid Sticks, he got another body, Lester Giles, the girl's landlord. He beat the man to death. That's how we found out where the girl is."

"Another body?" asked Simon, wiping the sweat from his brow.

"Yeah, looks that way. This kid Sticks, I don't know." Dizzy shook his head in silence, thinking of all the possible repercussions. "I think we need to get someone down there to get the girl."

"Go get the girl, get her back up here so she can testify."

Simon paused for a split second. "Leave him down there, buried somewhere down there. You understand, Dizzy."

"Say no more."

"No more said," said Simon, looking at his friend.

"Shit, it's hot in here. You better come on before your ass falls out."

Simon Shuller watched as Dizzy strolled out of the sauna. He closed his eyes and lay down on the wooden bench.

SCAREDY CAT

Fuck, it's dark as shit out here. Ain't no lights and shit. Nigga could come up missing out this motherfucker for real and never be found again. You should slow down."

"Man, ain't nothing out here. Stop whining. It's just darkness, that's all. Ain'tcho never been down South before?" asked Sticks, looking at Rayford Johnson, whom everyone referred to as Ray J, a simple nickname after his own birthright. Sticks didn't know much about him, except that he was a hustler and he hustled for Simon Shuller across town. He knew of the guy, but Sticks had never associated with him and knew very little about him, his people, and had not a clue where he came from or why he was there. *I could have handled this situation myself. Shit, I been handling everything. I don't know why they sent this clown-ass nigga along for the ride in the first place.*

They crossed the Virginia state line, and as at every state line, they passed the welcome sign on the side of the road. "Welcome to Tennessee."

"You got the map?" asked Sticks.

"Yeah, right here, let me see." Ray J picked up the map, turning it once in the upside position. "Looks like we stay right here on I-81, to Interstate 40 West, that's gonna run us right on into I-640 West and straight on into Nashville."

"All right, all right then, I-40 West, I got her address for you to find too. You can find her address on that map?" Sticks questioned, checking out Ray J's map skills.

"Yeah, of course, a map can always get you where you going."

From out of the darkness of the night, a flash of movement darted out in front of Sticks's car.

"Watch out!" screamed Ray J.

Sticks quickly slammed on the brakes, his lights blinding the fawn frozen still in the middle of the road. Sticks cut his wheel hard to the left. His right front end struck the animal, spinning his car in a 180-degree arc, as he lost control for a mere second, the car running off the road and into a ditch.

"What the fuck was that?" screamed Ray J, completely shook.

"I don't know, man, I think it was a deer or something," said Sticks, spinning the right-side tire as he tried to get out of the ditch.

"You gonna dig us in a hole and we ain't never gonna get outta here. I told you to slow down, you should've listened," said Ray J, looking around at the nothingness of the deserted countryside. The vast land stretched as far as the eye could see, but yet there was only green grass and heavily wooded areas of different types of oak and maples traveling alongside the interstate.

"Come on, let's get out and take a look," said Sticks.

Is this nigga crazy? I'm not getting out this car, it's too damn dark out here. "Hey, just go on back there and see if you can push her and I'll give it a little gas," said Ray J, sliding right over to the driver's seat, ready to put that motherfucker in reverse and run Sticks's ass over. *He lucky I don't have the girl yet, 'cause that's just what I'd do too, run his dumb ass over. Now we stuck out here in the middle of bubble fuck nowhere in the god damn dark with his dumb ass crashing into deer and shit.* It was scary, pitch black "can't see nothing but the twinkling of the stars in the sky" dark out there. Tennessee was backwoods at its finest, home of Davy Crockett and the birthplace of country music.

Sticks put his hands on the trunk of the car and began to push as Ray J stepped on the gas pedal, causing the tire to spin and dirt to fly up, hitting Sticks in the face and soiling his clothing.

"Hey, stop, man, you fucking me all up back here!" he huffed at Ray J, who put the car in park.

"What's the matter?" Ray J hollered out the window.

"Man, you got dirt flying everywhere back here. Wait a minute, the ground is way too soft," said Sticks, examining the hole the spinning tire had dug itself into. Just then car lights could be seen traveling a half-mile's distance down the road.

"Look, maybe we can get some help out here."

"Shit, with our luck fuck around and Jason pull up out this bitch, then what? KKK have us tied up out this motherfucker and won't nobody ever know and won't nobody ever find us."

"Yo, wait till we get back, man. I'm telling everybody yousa big-ass scaredy cat."

No you not, you won't be getting back to tell nobody nothing, thought Ray J.

NAME GAME

Are we still on for next Saturday with your parents?" asked Vivian, already thinking of the perfect tan dress for dinner at Le Bec Fin with Tommy's mom and dad.

"Oh, shit, I almost forgot, my parents are coming this week!" he exclaimed.

"Um, yeah, how can you forget that? So, I take it we're still on for dinner at Le Bec, right?" she asked, tossing cut tomatoes into a bowl filled with lettuce, cucumbers, and shaved carrots, while tossing her blond hair away from her face at the same time.

"Yeah, yeah, we're still on," mumbled Tommy, his mind now thinking of who he could possibly hire to clean up his apartment. God knows, if his mother took one look at his place in the condition it was in, he'd never hear the end of it. He could hear her now: "Dear God, Tommy, look at how you live. If I didn't know better I would swear a wild beast lives here and not my son. I didn't raise you to live like this." Then his father would add his two cents. "Margaret, please, leave the boy alone, he's a single man, he's living just fine." They would go back and forth and Tommy would never hear the end of it.

"Matty moved back home, you know," said Tommy as he set two places at the table.

"Are you serious, your parents let him move back in their house? Do you think they should have done that under the circumstances?" she asked, biting a sliced cucumber from out of a tossed salad.

"Probably not, but something tells me I'll never hear the end of it."

"Is he okay?" said Vivian placing the salad bowl on the table and setting a large spoon next to it.

"You know, I don't think Matty will ever be okay. But if he can stay clean, who knows," said Tommy, growing silent thinking of his brother, of the last time he saw him. It was Tommy who picked him up from Castle Rehabilitation after a drug overdose almost took his life seven months ago.

"You okay, Tommy? You look like you're out in space. Earth to Tommy, hello in there," she said, waving her hand in front of his eyes as she bent face to face with him, stared into his eyes, and kissed his lips softly. "Do you hear me, Tommy?"

"Yeah, Viv, I'm just thinking."

"Well, come on, think and eat. I got all your favorites, salad with Italian dressing, chicken parmigiana, with melted mozzarella, thin spaghetti and homemade gravy, and fresh cannolis for dessert that I picked up from your Uncle Vito's bakery."

"No way, you went down to Uncle Vito's?"

"Yeah, I did, just for you, Tommy, just for you," she said as she wrapped her arms around his neck. "I worry about you, Tommy, seriously."

"I know Viv, I know. I'm okay. I'm keeping it together. It's all good, no need to worry."

"What about work, what's going on with the Somerset Killer case?" she asked, letting him go and making her way back into the kitchen.

"Viv, you're killing me here. I don't want to talk about it."

"The newspaper said that trial had to be postponed because the witness whose identity was being withheld was missing."

"Yeah, another headache. Viv, really, I don't want to talk about work. I just want to have a nice, quiet night at home with you."

"Okay, fine, we don't have to talk about it." She paused for a moment. "I got the biggest break in one of my cases today. Seriously, Tommy, huge break, remember the bank case and everything, all those tedious hours of watching bank surveillance video? I swear you won't believe it. Finally, a real person, can you believe it. Some girl was stupid enough to walk into a bank, take fifty thousand dollars out, and use her real name. It's unbelievable. We got her real name, her real address, everything, and get this, guess what the best part is?"

"Viv, you know what, I don't care what the best part is. I told you I don't want to talk about work, not mine, not yours, not anything. Can't we just pretend for once that you're a secretary instead of an FBI agent? And how about we can pretend that I'm a former police detective, being as Captain Dan is going to have my badge if . . . I don't even want to talk about it," said Tommy, shaking off thoughts of the worst outcome possible. He couldn't help thinking about the murders he and his partner, Merva Ross, were unable to solve. While they had captured Bernard Guess and had him in custody awaiting trial, there was someone else out there leaving a string of dead bodies behind, and it all connected to the Somerset murders.

"Tommy, I'm sorry. Really, come on, sit down, let's just eat dinner. We don't have to talk, okay?" said Vivian, not wanting to upset him. Just as she sat down and asked him to pass the salad dressing, her pager went off.

"See, we can't even have a quiet dinner at home, just the two of us, Viv."

"Yes, we can. Let me just check in. It's Chambers."

Vivian picked up the phone and dialed Chambers back. She waited, the phone rang twice, he picked up. Tommy continued with dinner. Digging into the plate of chicken parmigiana, adding gravy to his spaghetti, he listened to a one-sided conversation.

"I knew she'd show up. They always do. I'm coming in. I want to make the arrest. I'll be there."

"A quiet meal together, just the two of us?" he questioned as he watched her hang up the phone.

"Tommy, my case, we've located this Fothergill character. I've got to go," she said, gathering her hair and pulling it back into a ponytail. *Did she just say Fothergill? Can't be, can't be the same person.* She ran into their bedroom and grabbed the Brics carry-on bag that she kept in the corner of her closet, packed and ready to go for great-escape emergencies such as this.

"You said Fothergill?" he questioned slyly.

Tommy stood still, watching her spin herself around her apartment like a Tasmanian devil. Within less than three minutes, she was at the door, Brics bag, purse, and lightweight jacket all in hand.

"Yeah, she cashed in on a fraudulent check and walked out of a bank with fifty thousand dollars."

"What's the name again?"

"Fothergill, um, like Daisy something or other. Here, kiss me, and don't be mad, I'll be back tomorrow."

"Mad, are you insane. I can't fucking believe you," he said, delighted, a complete personality change from the grumpy, disengaged boyfriend she had been having dinner with. He picked her up and kissed her. "Viv, she's the missing witness we've been looking for, the unidentified witness from the newspaper headlines. You don't know, Vivian, you just saved my ass. Come on, let's go, I have to bring her in, she has to get back here to testify."

"Wow, I thought you didn't want to talk about my work," she said with a hint of sarcasm.

"Are you nuts, I want to hear about your work every day from now on, baby. Oh, my god, Vivian, I fucking love you. You are the best, babe, the best, you know that? I could marry you right now," he said, grabbing her head and kissing her face.

"Well, aren't you the excited one. Come on, let's go get your *star* witness and then we can go look at rings," said Vivian, closing and locking her door behind them.

"Viv, I said I could marry you right now, I said nothing about later."

"Whatever, Tommy, whatever. Remember, um, don't you need your witness?"

"So, you want to shop for rings?"

"Do I?" she said, smiling again.

BUSTED

Daisy was busy in the kitchen making her first attempt at pre-paring Billy a home-cooked meal. He said his favorite was meatloaf and mashed potatoes, and that he could eat it every day of his life and be content. It was a simple meal for a simple man. However, it was turning out to be rather difficult for her to prepare. Poor Daisy had never attempted to cook for herself, let alone for a man. She had cut her finger twice trying to cut the skin off the potatoes, so instead, she was boiling them skin on. *We'll figure out how to get the skin off later or maybe we'll just have mashed potatoes and skin peelings.* Sounded like a good plan to her, besides, her momma always said all the vitamins and nutri-ents were in the skin anyway. The meatloaf would have turned out perfectly, had she not still had it in the oven cooking. A little dry, but ketchup would fix it. *Billy won't know the difference.*

Just then she heard him knocking at the door. Quickly she wiped her hands on a towel and opened the door, letting him come inside from the long hallway that led to the staircase.

"Hi, Daisy Mae," he said, sure and confident.

"Hey, Billy, come on in and make yourself right at home. Would you like some lemonade? I made it myself, fresh squeezed."

"I'll take a glass, thank you kindly," he said as he sat down on the sofa and reached for the remote. "You mind if I change this channel? It's football Sunday, Daisy Mae."

"I know, Billy, you tell me all the time. Go on ahead and change the channel," she said, removing her pot of boiling potatoes from the stove.

She opened the refrigerator door, realizing she had forgotten the sour cream. "Dagnabbit," she said, thinking of how important the sour cream was to the recipe for creamy homestyle mashed potatoes that she had gotten out of her *Southern Flavor Cook Book*, which she had purchased at the Barnes and Noble downtown. "I knew I forgot something. I swear sometimes I think I left my head on the bus," she said.

"What, Daisy, what happened?"

"I forgot the sour cream," she said, cursing herself.

"Well, I can run down to the market and get you some, if you want."

"No, Billy, you been working at the factory and what not, just go on and rest. I'll run down to the store, just go on and watch your football game," she said, grabbing her purse and car keys.

Sticks had just about had it with the South and wanted to go home. It had been two of the longest, hottest days he had ever experienced in his life. His travel companion offered no relief from the merciless heat that engulfed them. Sticks was stripped down to a dirty wife beater, dirty jeans, and dirty Adidas, and looked raggedy and withered, drained. The deer, the ditch, the tow, the Crazy 8 Motel they stayed in, Ray J, the diners with nothing on the menu but eggs over easy, biscuits, gravy, sausage, juice, water. That's it, don't ask for nothing else.

"Do you have turkey bacon, Ethel?" asked Sticks, reading Ethel's name tag and wondering how she got her hair to stand up in a beehive bun on top of her head.

"No, it's not on the menu, sir," she said, like a robot woman with bright blue eye shadow on her eyelids and cherry-red lipstick painted on her mouth.

"Just runny eggs, sausage, biscuits, and gravy?" he asked, apparently talking to himself, as she stood there waiting for his order. "I wanted pancakes, no pancakes?" he asked, realizing he was in hillbilly hell.

"No, it's not on the menu, sir."

"That's because there's nothing on the menu in this motherfucker," he said, sliding the menu across the countertop at her and walking out.

That was actually a couple of hours ago and he still had not eaten. Sticks and Ray J pulled into the Shalat Apartment Homes. The investigator had done a thorough search, leaving no stone unturned and delivering valuable and precise information to Simon Shuller.

"Let me see here," said Sticks, looking at the piece of paper Simon Shuller had handed him. "Okay, she's in apartment 1805."

It was all about to go down. He parked his car around the back of the building. They got out of the car and Ray J checked his .45, tucking it into the back of his pants. "Let's go get this done with," he said to Sticks.

"Let's do it," Sticks agreed, and led the way with Ray J close behind. They got up to the apartment and walked to the door marked 1805. Sticks knocked at the door, then stepped to the side.

"Damn, you sure was quick about it," said Billy as he opened the door. "What you do, fly to the . . ." he said as he swung the door back to the unfamiliar faces in front of him. No one said a word. Everyone exchanged quick glances, Ray J eyeing the inside of the apartment for others.

"Is Daisy here?" asked Sticks.

Unthinkingly, Billy answered him. "Well, she's not here right now. But she'll be back."

That was all Ray J had to hear. He had found his mark; it was time for some action. He pulled his .45 from behind his back and held it at point-blank range in Billy's face.

"Hey, what's going on here?" Billy asked, oblivious, being backed into the apartment, the door closing behind the three of them.

"Who the fuck are you?" asked Sticks.

"Nobody, I'm nobody," said Billy, scared to death and about to pee on himself. He had never had a gun pointed at him. *God, please don't let them kill me.*

"What the fuck you doing here, nobody?" questioned Ray J, as Sticks looked around the apartment for signs that someone else was there.

"I'm just visiting," said Billy, trembling on the inside.

"Where's Daisy?" asked Sticks.

Billy stood in silence for a minute as he thought about everything that was going on. As scared as he was, he'd just have to face the unknown, but there was no way he was telling these guys that Daisy was down the road at Wibler's Market. One thing for sure, two things for certain, Daisy was in a world of trouble with the likes of these guys looking for her, and Billy knew they were here to bring her no good.

"Nobody, where's Daisy?" asked Ray J, poking his side with the gun.

"I can't tell you that," he said, knees trembling.

"What did you just say?" asked Sticks as he turned around, frowned, and busted Billy in the face with his right hand, dead on his jaw. Billy fell back but caught himself before falling. "I know you ain't protecting this whore. I'm gonna ask you one more time, where the fuck is Daisy?"

Billy knew they meant business. He prayed and prayed that she didn't walk back through that door. He didn't want to see her hurt. Before he could even think about responding, he found himself the target of a brutal beating. On the floor, in a fetal position, he was kicked and stomped down. His head was bleeding, blood was dripping from his mouth, his shoulder was completely dislocated from the stomping, and two of his ribs were broken.

"I'm gonna ask you one more time. Where's the girl?" said Ray J, bending down and putting the gun in Billy's face once again.

Billy had already seen his life flash in front of his eyes, all twenty-six years of his life. Ray J stuck the barrel of the gun in Billy's mouth. "Nigga, I'll blow your brains out, you fucking understand me? Answer me," said Ray J, ready to kill him.

Sticks really wanted to make it back home. He damn sure didn't want to get jammed up down South.

"Whoa, calm down, man," he said, nodding to Ray J to be easy. Then he added, "What the fuck is you protecting her for, she's a whore, everybody fucked her."

Billy lay still on the ground listening to Sticks as his eyes shot daggers of death at him.

"What you like her? You getting mad 'cause I'm talking about your ho? Y'all in here playing whorehouse and shit, I see somebody in there cooking and shit. Man, don't you know, you can't turn no whore into a housewife. Shit just won't work," said Sticks. Tears fell from Billy's eyes as he listened to Sticks slander and degrade Daisy. He was in so much pain, his side hurt more than his head and he could feel that one of his teeth on the upper top right side was loose. All he could do was lie still on the floor, holding his side tightly with both his arms, trying to protect the area in case they hit him again.

"Man, hog-tie this motherfucker," said Ray J, reaching into a bag he had carried from the car, and throwing a roll of rope to Sticks. "Tie him up tight too," said Ray J, his gun in hand.

Sticks thought nothing of it, caught the rope in midair, put his gun down, and rolled Billy onto his stomach, showing no mercy. Billy screamed in agonizing pain as Sticks began to tie him up, folding his wrists behind his back and using the rope to secure them. After his wrists he tied his feet together at the ankles. Then, before he could turn around and tie Billy's ankles to his wrists he felt the barrel of cold steel pressed against the back right side of his head. He looked down at Ray J's feet, standing right behind him, about to take his life.

"Simon Shuller sends his best regards," said Ray J, and he pulled the trigger, taking the shot, the perfect shot. Sticks raised his head just in time to see it coming, rather than never knowing what hit him. He knew it was coming, death, and the grim reaper was a tall, light-skinned, big, solid-built nigga named Rayford Johnson. Sticks, shocked at first, looked over his shoulder at Ray J, then his hand felt the back of his head, and he could feel his body falling to lie next to Billy's, then darkness.

"Aww, damn, mister, please don't kill me, please. I won't say a word," said Billy as the keys to the door could be heard on the other side. It was Daisy coming back from the store. She opened the door and walked straight into the kitchen, never even looking into the living room.

"Hey, Billy, I'm back," she said, setting her things on the counter. She turned the corner and her eyes widened to the size of golf balls. "Billy, oh, my god," she screamed, "are you okay?" She ran to him.

"Watch out, Daisy," said Billy as Ray J grabbed her. Daisy struggled as Ray J tightened his grip around her body with one arm, his free hand around her neck, choking her as he pressed his body against hers. "I remember you, from the Honey Dipper, right?" he questioned checking out her face real good. "Shit, I almost didn't recognize you with your clothes on. Damn, you had a nice body, girl, and a pretty pussy. I always did want to fuck you. I missed that damn party though, the bachelor party. I heard though. I heard all about you. You take a lot of dick, baby. Damn, you fine." Daisy whimpered as she looked over at Billy. He looked beat up real bad. His head was swollen and blood was still dripping from his mouth.

He looked up at Ray J holding a gun to Daisy's side with his arm still wrapped around her, while his free hand began to fondle her body.

"Please, stop, I don't do that no more," she said, fighting his hand off.

"Bitch, is you crazy?" questioned Ray J, smacking Daisy in the face three times with his free hand. She couldn't block him or duck him. And then he grabbed her hair, pulled her close to him, and looked her dead in the eyes. "You fucked everybody and you begging me please, looking at me like I'm disgusting you. You gonna beg me please, all right. Let's go." Daisy stood emotionless, the gun and the circumstances consuming her. Her past was right here in her face and as numb as she had been all those years, she was just as numb standing there in the living room of her present.

"Come on, we got to go, you got court," said Ray J.

"Get off her," hollered out Billy, tied and unable to do anything.

"Damn, shut the fuck up, nigga," Ray J said, before turning around and firing one bullet to silence him. It seemed as though she heard him, after he was shot, or maybe it was the single shot that broke her reverie.

"Billy, noooo! Oh, God, please, no, Billy," she screamed, trying to break free from Ray J as Billy lay on the floor in a pool of blood.

"Bitch, say one word and I'll kill you, too. Shut up!" he commanded, grabbing her hair as he dragged her across the floor.

He made her reach down into Sticks's pockets and get the keys to the car outside. "Hurry up about it, and come on," he ordered. That was all he needed, his business here was complete, and upon returning home, he'd collect a king-sized ransom for a hard day's work.

Just as he opened the door and stepped out of the apartment, he saw Agent Lang and Agent Chambers turning the corner and heading toward them.

"Daisy Mae Fothergill, FBI!" Agent Lang yelled out. She took one look at Daisy and recognized her from the video surveillance from the bank. The suspect was only four hundred feet away. Just as she began to reach for her piece, Ray J like lightning began firing at them.

"Watch out!" yelled Chambers as he pushed Lang into the safety of a doorway that was two feet inside the hallway, body pressing her away from harm. He peeked around the tiny corner of the cubby entrance. The coast was clear.

"Come on," he said, nodding to Lang as gunshots could be heard from outside. Tommy had given strict orders that there was to be no exchange of gunfire that could hurt his star witness. An FBI agent, using a bullhorn, was offering fake assurances to Ray J, who was hiding behind a tree and using Daisy as a human shield. Ray J quickly took out his clip and replaced it, fully loaded and ready.

"I got him, I got a clear shot," an agent could be heard through the headpiece plugged into Delgado's ear.

"Take him," he said, believing the kid would make the shot.

But as his aim was off by two inches, and there was a sudden movement by Ray J himself, the sniper hit dead on his shoulder bone, shattering it into a thousand pieces inside his flesh.

"Aaahhh!" Daisy screamed for help as Ray J took the hit to his shoulder, letting her go, screaming in pain. He reached for his arm, and another bullet pierced his chest cavity, knocking him back onto the ground, where he crawled against the tree. The sniper from the roof zeroed in on Ray J, looking through the scope of his rifle. Ray J no longer had Daisy to use as a human shield. He was outnumbered and he knew it. He lifted his gun and pointed it at Daisy. The gunshot seemed surreal. Tommy Delgado fired it right above Daisy's head, taking the chance she wouldn't interrupt its path. Daisy turned around to see Ray J with his gun in hand, pointed at her, and a bullet hole right between his eyes, before he fell back onto the ground right beside her.

"It's my favorite shot," he shouted, looking at Daisy, who looked as if she was about to faint. "Daisy Mae Fothergill?" he asked.

Unable to speak, she shook her head yes. Delgado held out his hand, helped her up.

"I'm Detective Delgado, do you remember me?"

Daisy softly shook her head yes again.

"We talked a while back. I'm here now and I'm going to take care of you. Everything will be all right," he said as a broken and frightened Daisy Mae began to cry in his arms. "It's okay, we're going back home now."

BANKING BUSINESS

Bobby DeSimone entered CFCF on State Road. Politely, he held the door for a young black girl pushing a baby stroller. *I would never want my kids to come through the door of this place, even if it were to visit me.* And he meant it. This was no place for children. No place at all for them. He bypassed the waiting line, walked over to a desk, and spoke with a corrections officer who politely escorted him to a private waiting area.

"Probably be about twenty minutes. They just finished up count. I'll let the CO on his block know you're here."

Within fifteen minutes, Bernard Guess was being seated at a table in a room where DeSimone was waiting for him.

"I didn't know you were coming," he said, as he placed his handcuffed wrists on the table in front of him.

"Me neither, kid, but something's come up. The police got the girl."

"I don't understand," said Nard.

"I called Sticks and his girlfriend claimed that him and some guy named Ray J—do you know him?"

"No," responded Nard, unfamiliar with the name.

"Well, they were both killed in a shootout with the police down in Murfreesboro, Tennessee."

"What were they doing there?" said Nard, as he thought of the consequences of Sticks's death. *Damn, not Sticks, that was my man.*

"I don't know, but one of my sources claims that the girl was taken into custody after the shootout with the police."

"So, what does that mean?"

"Well, it means that I can't speak to her. It means that I can't confirm that she's giving us an alibi, and then this morning, I get a call from the DA's office. They took the case down to manslaughter and offered you a plea bargain of fifteen to twenty years, eligible for parole in eight."

Is he insane, I'm not taking no plea deal. The girl got the alibi for me. What's wrong with him, is he trying to hang me? He just don't want to do the work.

"Hell, no, is you crazy. I'm not doing no fucking eight years," said Nard, pounding his hands on the table. "I got an alibi, the girl told you, she told the investigator, it's done. Sticks told me not to worry."

"Yeah, but Sticks is dead now and I can't talk to this girl. I just think that if there's a chance—"

"Man, look, I'm not taking no plea deal. Fuck fifteen to twenty. What kind of deal is that anyway? There's no chance I'd make parole in eight years. I'm stuck. Naw, I know for certain what my man Sticks said, and he said we had nothing to worry about. He said the girl was straight and he took care of her. She's definitely going to do the right thing."

"You're willing to take that chance?"

"What choice do I got? That plea bargain shit you got ain't no option."

"It's just that I think—"

"No, I think you need to realize I'm not doing no prison time. Listen, I got an alibi. I got the girl. She's going to do the right thing, trust me. Her testimony is in the bag, Sticks told me not to worry."

"So, you want me to turn the deal down."

"Fuck that deal, I'm not going to jail. Watch, everything is going to work out."

Bobby DeSimone looked at Nard and even he himself began to believe in his confidence.

"You're right, if you got the alibi then why plead out anyway, right?"

"Right."

Daisy was taken into police protective custody where she would remain. The police, after what had happened in Tennessee, felt it better to be safe than sorry. Daisy had returned with Agents Lang and Chambers and was under their protection. It turns out that the bank error she thought was a bank error wasn't an error at all. She was a cohost in the biggest counterfeit check scam that the banking industry had seen. Over $70 million in counterfeit checks had been passed over the last five years and here finally was the missing link.

"Hi, Daisy, can I get you some coffee, juice, soda, water,

perhaps?" asked Agent Lang as she closed the door behind her and seated herself at her desk.

"Um, no, I'm fine," said Daisy. "Thank you, though."

"So, Daisy, what happened to the fifty thousand dollars you took out of the bank."

Daisy was completely caught off guard. She didn't know what to say. She didn't want to give it back. She needed that money so she wouldn't have to strip or dance again.

"Well, I spent it, I guess."

"Fifty thousand dollars, you spent it, in less than two months?"

"Mmm hmm," she said, lying through her teeth.

"What did you spend it on?"

"Well, I sort of spent it on a bunch of stuff."

"Do you know whose money that is, Daisy?" asked Vivian, curious to hear her answer.

"Well, I guess it belongs to the bank."

"Where did the check come from?"

"I don't know, I never saw no check."

"So, you just woke up one morning and decided to go take fifty thousand dollars out of the bank that you knew wasn't yours."

"Well, I thought the bank made some kind of error and yeah, I woke up and went on down to the bank and got the money. I still don't know what I did wrong."

"Have you ever seen this check before?"

"No," said Daisy, staring at a check in the amount of fifty thousand dollars.

"Is that your signature?"

"No, ma'am, not mine."

"This check is counterfeit."

"Well, if it's counterfeit, why'd the bank give me the money?"

"At the time, they didn't know. I want you to do me a favor. I want you to look at the bank's video surveillance and I want you to tell me if you recognize anyone in the bank."

Vivian Lang walked around her desk to a television that was sitting kitty-corner in her office on a steel rack. She grabbed the remote, sat on the corner of her desk, and pressed play. Daisy watched patiently as an old woman walked into the bank, with Reggie Carter, her missing man.

"Oh, my God, that's Reggie, and that's his . . . his mom."

"His mother?" questioned Lang.

"Yeah, his mom."

This case was getting weirder and weirder by the second. They finished looking at the tapes and Daisy just couldn't believe it. Reggie and his mother had a counterfeit check they put in her account. She watched the tape of the old woman coming into the bank trying to take the money, and leaving rather hastily on finding out the account was frozen.

"They must have gotten scared and left after hearing your account was frozen," said Lang, throwing the possibility out in the air to see Daisy's reaction. Truth hurts, and the look on Daisy's face said she was in agonizing pain.

"Must have," said Daisy, shocked and embarrassed that Reggie was a bank thief, not the businessman she thought he was.

"When is the last time you saw him?" asked Lang, marking the date on her notepad. It was actually the same day he made the bank deposit. *Poor girl, I wonder does she get the picture like*

I do, thought Lang. It wouldn't take a rocket scientist to figure out. He was only using her.

Daisy sat still, thinking to herself, unable to believe that Reggie Carter was just a lie. *But I thought he loved me.* Once the bank said the account was frozen, he had no choice but to roll out; he thought the FBI and the bank were on to him. But Reggie thought wrong. The FBI and the bank weren't on to him. They were on to Daisy. The only reason Daisy's account had been frozen was that she had been cashing Abigail's Social Security checks. The problem was Abigail was dead. When the government finally did receive the death certificate, they immediately credited that money back to the government, charging the bank. The bank then went after Daisy for the money, freezing the account and marking her in the hole. So, when Reggie came along and got her banking information, and then deposited the check, the check cleared, but the account was frozen. Once Daisy realized she was fifty thousand dollars richer and went into the bank, the freeze was lifted, and she was given the money minus her debt to the bank. Agent Lang's video surveillance showed it all.

"That's Reggie Carter," said Daisy. "That's him right there."

It would be proven later that his name wasn't Reggie Carter at all, but Jackson Fontaine. The woman who she thought to be his mother, the one he had introduced as his mother, really wasn't. She was the "check maker," the actual key to the entire operation. Reggie's talent lay in knowing how to target the unsuspecting. He knew all along what she did for a living— that's why he targeted her; he wanted sex. He wasn't lacking in mental acuity by any means. He robbed banks and got away free, clean, and clear—until Daisy Mae, that is. She was the first real link to a name and a face that Agent Lang had throughout the entire database.

And with all the information that Daisy had on him, she would prove to be a valuable resource for Agents Lang and Chambers. It was a long, sordid, ugly scenario, and once Daisy looked at the videotapes and got a full understanding of the situation, she was overwhelmed with grief. *I really thought he loved me.* When she told her story to Agent Lang, how she quit her job, was house hunting, and really thought he was going to marry her, even Agent Lang felt remorseful.

"Listen, this is a lesson. You live, you learn. Don't beat yourself up, okay. I just need you to do one more thing for me, Daisy."

She sat Daisy in a room with a piece of paper and a pen, cameras secretly rolling. "I need you to sign this paper for me one hundred times, okay?"

"Just my mother's name?"

"Yup, that's it, just your mother's name." Agent Lang smiled at her as she closed the door. She walked no more than a yard away, opened a door, and stood next to her partner as they watched Daisy signing her mother's signature through a mirrored wall.

"If this girl fails the stenography test, I will put her in the penitentiary myself," said Lang.

"Yeah, I'm hoping she didn't sign that check too. I sort of feel sorry for her, so far her story pans out and everything she's told us about this Carter character has been right on point. She was the missing link," said Chambers.

"We'll see. I hope so," Lang added, watching Daisy through the glass wall.

Lang rushed the signature pages to be analyzed by a team of handwriting specialists. Tommy paced up and down the floor.

"I'm telling you, Viv, she's telling the truth, I can feel it. She didn't know what that scumbag was doing. He was just using her, that's it."

"You bet on your gut, I'm strictly science and what can be proven," said Vivian. "But I do hope you're right this time, Tommy Delgado," she said, placing a call to Chambers to see if he'd heard anything yet.

Sure enough, the finding was that Daisy did not endorse the counterfeit check. Had that been the case, Daisy would have been going to prison for a really long time. Be that as it may, the fact that she cooperated with Agents Lang and Chambers and helped them in their investigation freed and cleared her and the debt of fifty thousand dollars that was owed to the bank was mysteriously wiped out of the system and marked paid. By the time Agents Lang and Chambers were ready to release Daisy from their custody, Detectives Tommy Delgado and Merva Ross were patiently waiting for her.

"You ready, kid?" asked Tommy.

"No, not really," said Daisy, knowing that she was about to testify and then go into police protective custody. Her life would never be the same. She thought of everything that had happened, all because she gave the alibi. *I miss my family, I miss Tennessee,* she thought, wondering if she'd ever see either again.

"Don't worry, it'll be a piece of cake," assured Merva, placing her hand on Daisy's shoulder, escorting her out of the federal building and into the back of an unmarked police car with tinted wondows.

STANDING OVATION

Daisy looked around the courtroom at the rows and rows of people as she was led in from a private back room. It would be the same room that she would be escorted back to before being transferred out and relocated into police protective custody. She had been rehearsed for countless hours by the district attorney's office. And she had grappled with herself for days about what in her heart she knew she had to do. For her it was do or die. And at the rate she was going, she would be dead, if not for Tommy Delgado and Vivian Lang. After the shootout at the Shalat Apartment Homes, Daisy really feared for her life. And why should she not? Right now, she was the target, she was the alibi, she was the one being put on display, and she was the one most sought after. The judge had refused to allow the use of cameras or video and ordered all media to stand outside. Even newspaper journalists were barred from his courtroom. When faced with testimony from those in police protective custody, the judge always used precautions. Today's testimony would be made of record and dispersed to the media by the judge's law clerk after the stenographer transcribed it.

Daisy was led to the stand, her eyes bouncing around the courtroom, desperately trying to find a focus. She was so nervous she had tears in her eyes. She didn't know if she could go through with it, but she was yearning for it to be over. She was nervous, so nervous she felt her stomach churning, and her mouth began to water as she climbed the steps and sat in the chair. She remembered what Detective Ross had said to her.

"Don't look at him. Don't make any eye contact with him. Stare away from him. I don't want him looking at you all crazy, trying to intimidate you, right, Tommy?" asked Merva as they were prepping her one last time in the tiny courthouse room.

"Yeah, she's right, this guy is a creep. Don't look at him at all, okay, kid?" he said, realizing that she was just a kid, a twenty-two-year-old kid, who had gotten herself in the worst trouble imaginable.

"Will you stand and place your hand on the Bible?" And of course she did, glancing over at the rows of jurors, twenty-four eyeballs all glued on her.

"Is the testimony that you are about to give today the truth, the whole truth, and nothing but the truth?" The question rang in her mind as her hand lay on the Bible. She had not seen a Bible since her days at the Trinity Spirit Worship House, and she thought back to all the peace and solace she had found in Tennessee.

"Yes, it is," she said assuredly.

"You may be seated."

Daisy sat down as the district attorney who had briefed her walked over to the podium where she was seated. Daisy chose to make the sheriff standing at the back door her focal point. She would look at the door, the sheriff, and the district attorney.

"Would you state your name for the record, please?"

"Daisy Mae Fothergill," said Daisy as she glanced over at the jurors once again.

"Okay, on the night of November 5, 1986, where were you?"

"I believe I was working that night," said Daisy, her apprehension subsiding.

"And where did you work at?"

"At the time, I was working at the Honey Dipper."

"What kind of work did you do at the Honey Dipper, Ms. Fothergill?"

"I was a stripper and an exotic dancer."

"On the night of November 5, 1986, do you recall seeing this man, a patron at the Honey Dipper?"

Daisy paused as her eyes met Nard's, which were fixed on her in a silent plea. Daisy quickly turned her head, remembering what Detective Ross had said.

"No, I do not recall seeing him there," she said, poised and composed.

It was at that moment, it was those words, it was unbelievable, to say the least, but all Nard's hopes and dreams escaped him, there was a lump in his throat, and he couldn't swallow, he couldn't think. *This isn't supposed to be happening. That's not what the fuck that bitch is supposed to be saying. What the fuck is she doing? What part of the game is this? What the fuck, Sticks, this bitch is drowning me. She's selling me the fuck out!* His eyes drew small as he watched her breathe every word she spoke against him. *How can she? Sticks said it would be okay. What is she doing? What the fuck is going on?* His head began to spin and his heart began to pound. He couldn't believe everything he had been told was a lie. He thought he had an alibi. He thought he was walking out of the courtroom. He thought he was straight.

"Have you ever seen the defendant before today?"

"No, I have not," said Daisy, recanting her previous statement to the private investigator that had been hired by Simon Shuller on behalf of Bernard Guess, as the jurors and the others in the courtroom buzzed with disbelief. Her testimony had just sunk the entire case for the defendant.

"No more questions, Your Honor."

The judge nodded and then looked at Bobby DeSimone. "Your witness," he said, wondering if DeSimone would be injudicious enough to question her.

"Just a few questions, Your Honor, just a few.

"Ms. Fothergill, you say today that you never saw my client before, is that correct?"

"Yes."

"However, this is your signature, is that correct?" he asked, as he swiftly walked back over to his table and picked up an investigative report marked as Exhibit A.

"Yes," Daisy Mae calmly responded.

"Your Honor, I would like this to be marked as Exhibit A," he said, handing the document over to the judge.

"In this document you state that the defendant was with you on the night in question, is that correct?"

"Yes."

"So, now today you've changed your mind and you want us to believe that you were lying then?" he asked, his eyebrows arched, giving her and the jurors the *Colbert Report* staredown.

"I was paid to say what I said."

"So you can be bought, is that your answer, Ms. Fothergill?"

"Objection, Your Honor, completely inappropriate," said the district attorney, quickly standing up and facing the court.

"Sustained. Watch it, Mr. DeSimone."

"For the record, just one more question here. Today, why should we believe you? If you'll lie once you'll lie twice."

"No, I've told the truth here today."

"Sure no one paid you to say what you've said, Ms. Fothergill?"

"Objection, Your Honor."

"Sustained."

"No more questions," said DeSimone, strolling over to his chair and seating himself behind the table.

Even with DeSimone's tricky and clever line of questioning, Nard's heart continued to sink, along with his fate. He bent his head down and stared into his lap. *She didn't do it, she didn't give me the alibi.* He looked at DeSimone, and a look of "sorry" was all over his face. *I swear I thought this bitch had me covered. What the fuck am I going to do now?*

"Will you be re-examining, Mr. Zone?"

"Yes, thank you, Your Honor."

"Ms. Fothergill, you said that you were paid to make the statements you formerly made to the private investigator hired on behalf of the defendant, correct?"

"Yes."

"Did anyone bribe you, or pay you today?"

"No."

"The statements that you have made today, you've made of your own free will."

"Yes, that is correct."

"Are you absolutely positive the defendant was not with you on the night in question?"

"I'm positive. He was not with me on the night in question."

"No more questions, Your Honor."

"You may step down, Ms. Fothergill," the judge said as Daisy stood up and stepped down three stairs to the floor of the courtroom.

She glanced at Nard's face. He scowled at her, a look of boiling hate. *I know you don't think it's over, bitch. One day I'll be back, and I'll get you for what you've done to me.*

Daisy made her way off the stand, all the while telling herself, *I should have never been involved with this. I should have never given that alibi statement to the investigator.* Daisy really felt that in her heart.

Tommy was standing next to the bailiff, who led them both back into the small room down the hall from the judge's chambers.

"How did I do?" was the first question she asked.

"You did great, Daisy. I couldn't have done better. He tried to come at you on the cross, but you stayed composed, you know."

"I was so scared. At first I didn't think I could speak," she said as she sat down at the table, Tommy pulling up a chair and seating himself next to her.

"You did really great, really great. Everything's going to be okay. The state is going to take care of you, Daisy. You'll be relocated in the next seventy-two hours and you'll be able to start a new life for yourself. You are really blessed to be alive. You know, I see a lot working as a detective; me and Ross both do. And you've been through a lot. I want you to work with the liaison that will be assigned to following through your relocation. Make sure you get some counseling, okay, kid?"

"Mmmm hmmm," said Daisy.

"Listen, life is crazy, we get caught up sometime, just take care of yourself out there and don't get caught up in nothing no more. *Capice?*"

"Yeah, *capice*," she said, smiling back at Tommy.

He was so cool, and so down to earth, like a cousin or a friend or something. He was the only man she had ever met who talked to her . . . like he really cared. Just as a friend, the way he treated her, meant a lot.

There was a knock at the door and they both looked up from the table. A white man appeared at the door, young, brown-haired, with glasses. He gave a nod to Tommy.

"Uhh, Daisy, I think someone is here to see you; wait one minute," Tommy said as he got up and opened the door wider, and standing behind the detective were Billy and her cousin Kimmie Sue.

"Hey, Daisy Mae," said Kimmie Sue as she hugged her cousin tightly. "Are you okay? My, you just don't know, we've been worried sick about you."

"What are you guys doing here?" she said, looking at Billy.

"Coming to make sure you're all right, that's what family and friends are for, right?" he asked her as he stared deeply into her eyes, wondering if she knew how much he had fallen in love with her.

"I think I'll just step outside and give you two a few minutes," said Kimmie Sue as she walked out, closing the door behind her.

"Oh, Billy, I'm so sorry," she said, so embarrassed at the thought of the last time she'd seen him and so ashamed for all the pain she had caused him. "Look at you, you're all bandaged up," she said. Her face began to crumble and her heart grew heavy, and a flood of tears poured from her eyes and down her face.

"Oh, now, Daisy Mae, I'll be all right. The doctor said in a couple of weeks, I'll be good as new. My shoulder's a little tore up from that gunshot, and I got some broken ribs. You just can't hug on me too tight, that's all," he said with the most charming of smiles.

"I never meant for you to get hurt. You were the best thing that ever come into my life, Billy Bob Porter," she said covering her face as she began to snivel.

"Please don't cry, Daisy Mae," Billy said, passing her his handkerchief.

"I'm sorry, I feel so bad, I'm just so sorry, Billy," she said, looking into his eyes, hoping he truly knew how sorry she was.

"Here, I got you something, Daisy Mae. I never had a chance to give it to you, 'cause you ran off to the store and when you come back, all hell had broke loose, but . . . here you go." He reached into his pocket and pulled out a small black box. "This here is for you," he said, extending his arm and handing the box to her.

Slowly she opened it. "Billy, I can't take this," she said, looking at him, confused.

"What do you mean, Daisy Mae. Don't you like it?"

"Billy, I have to go away, to police protective custody, and they say once I leave, I'll never be able to come back," she said, breaking down and beginning to cry again.

"I know. That's why I'm so glad we got here before you had to go. Kimmie Sue said something like that, but Daisy, you're the first girl I've ever loved and that there is your ring from me."

"But I don't deserve it," she said, crying and covering her face again.

"Of course you do. I love you, Daisy Mae, you're my girl, and I know in my heart that you always will be. I wish you could stay, but I don't want you in harm's way and I cain't protect you like the law will, so I know you got to go. I just want you to take that ring and every time you look at it just say somewhere out there I know Billy Porter is, and he loves me with all his heart and I'll be okay with that," he said, bringing her to tears.

"Oh, Billy, I love you too. I don't know what I'm gonna do without you," she said, as he comforted her, holding her close as he rubbed her head and shoulders and told her everything would be okay.

"It'll be okay," said Billy reassuringly, looking into her eyes. "You're going to be okay; these people are going to protect you now."

She smiled and somehow, even though nothing was right in her life, she knew it would be.

"I love you, Daisy Mae."

Dizzy walked into the back of Fabulous Willie Man's barber shop. He sat down at a table and nodded for one of the stock boys to bring him his usual, cold bottled Evian water. Dizzy drank only Evian water and he drank it all day long. He believed it was keeping him alive.

"So, the girl didn't testify?" asked Simon.

"Nope, according to her testimony she wasn't paid to testify. Inside sources sayin' Sticks never gave her that fifty thousand. He kept it and gave her his Cadillac Seville and bought him a new Mercedes."

"I'm glad we left his ass in Tennessee."

"Yeah, he's not coming back, and as for the girl, they're saying she's not coming back either. They say she went into police protective custody."

"You want me to trace her?"

"Naw, for what, she don't owe us nothing, let her go," said Simon, thinking in overdrive. "And Nard?" asked Simon curiously.

"Well, they say he'll be shipped out to Green in the next twenty-four hours to start serving his sentence. DeSimone says the possibility of an appeal getting granted looks good, real good. You know it's rough in Green, but I've already told our people out there to watch out for him when he comes through."

"What about his mother, his family, are they straight?"

"Oh, yeah, they're good, I took care of them last week, I did everything Nard asked be done."

"And the kid never snitched?" asked Simon.

"Naw, he never said a word."

"They don't make them like that these days."

"They sure don't," said Dizzy, wishing more soldiers were built like Nard.

"So, now what's left to do now that all the smoke has cleared and the dust has settled?"

"Hell if I know, but before the day is over I'll bet it'll be something. Come on, let's get our tickets and go to the Sixers game; feel like some basketball tonight, floor seats, it don't get no better," said Dizzy.

"If ain't nothing else to do, I guess we might as well," said Simon, picking himself up out of the chair. "Old age is an ugly beast, my friend," said Simon, feeling a little stiff.

"Sure is," said Dizzy, "but hey, they got them cheerleaders, they'll make you feel young again," joked Dizzy, feeling the spirit as the thought of them jumping around and bending over in front of him entered his mind.

"Yeah, sure they will."

"Hey, Viv, how about acey deucy. Feel like getting your ass kicked tonight?" said Tommy, pulling the backgammon board from under the sofa.

"Tommy, you can't beat me. What the fuck is wrong with you, have you been hanging out with your brother Matty or what? You on drugs, Tommy? I'll kick your ass all up and down this backgammon board. Come on, put some money on it—I can lay away my ring when I win," she said, smacking his face playfully as he pushed her down on her back and began kissing her neck and behind her ears.

"Tommy, I thought you wanted to play."

"I am, what do you think I'm doing over here, Viv, hanging wall flowers?" he said, kissing her mouth and using his free arm to reach over and cut out the light.

"Do you love me?" Vivian asked, unsure of him at times.

"What the fuck, Viv, you hanging out with Matty or what? Of course, I love you. You're my life."

"I need a ring."

"I'll get you one tomorrow."

"Really?"

"Really, now come on, acey my deucy over here and stop playing games."

THE END

THE END

READING GROUP GUIDE

1. Did you the reader think that Daisy should have given Nard the alibi? Why?

2. Did she do the right thing by not testifying on his behalf?

3. Do you think Daisy would be considered a snitch for not giving the alibi?

4. What do you think happened to Reggie Carter?

5. Who do you think Daisy Mae Fothergill was pregnant by?

6. Do you think she should have kept the baby or do you agree with her decision to have the abortion?

7. Do you think that she and Billy would have gotten married if no one found her in Murfreesboro, Tennessee?

8. What would her mother have said if she were alive?

9. How many deaths were there related to the alibi in this book?

10. What should Daisy have done differently?

11. How can other young girls learn from her?

**Daisy thought she could hide
from her past forever.
She was wrong . . .**

Please turn the page
for a preview of

ALIBI II

Available in 2011

2006

THE COMEBACK

Diana Praeliou emerged from the kitchen patio. "It's absolutely beautiful out today," she said to her husband as he kissed her cheek. "A perfect day for a hot air balloon ride," she said, like a kid wanting a lollipop in a candy store.

"I wish I could, but you know I'm out of here today."

"Oh, yeah, that," she said, having completely forgotten. "I remember, you did say that you had a convention in Miami, and next month, the Doctrine of Medical Excellence Ceremony, which I'm shopping for a dress to wear to as we speak."

"I know my schedule is tight."

"You think?" she asked sarcastically. "Do you think you could pencil me in for a quiet dinner alone, just the two of us?"

"Someone has to pay the bills around here, Diana."

"This is true, and you do a wonderful job, honey," she said jokingly, wrapping her arms around him.

"Do you remember the first time I ever hugged you?" he asked, as he lovingly stared into his wife's eyes.

The first time we hugged. Only he would remember the first time we hugged. Jeez, he always does this to me.

"Hmmm, now let me see, darling," she said, playing for more time.

"You don't remember. I might as well tell you."

"No, I do, I do, wait," she said, as her husband began fidgeting and tickling at her sides.

"I know, stop that, our first hug, body to body, was at the game. Remember, the Hawks won the game seven to zero, remember, and I was there and I ran down on the field and you hugged me, swung me around, and squeezed the living daylights out of me, in all that heavy armor you was wearing, all big and strong," she said, batting her perfectly fitted eyelashes at him as she felt his hand sliding down her back and into the middle of her legs.

"Now," she said, as she passionately kissed him.

"Now," he said, as he lay down on top of her, simply destroying her first attempt at getting dressed for the day. They passionately made love as they did most mornings, a perfect start to every waking day they spent together. Webster came inside his wife, taking less than five minutes from start to finish, but leaving Diana with a feeling that could last an eternity.

"I wish you didn't have to go," she said, smiling as she wrapped her arms around her husband and moved her leg in between his, holding on to him as if to let him go would be to let go her last breath.

"I wish I didn't have to go either, but can you wait for Spain or what?" he asked, kissing the tip of her nose.

"No, no, I absolutely can't. Spain is going to simply be the best, our twentieth wedding anniversary and we're going to see the bull fighting. Oh, my God, Webster, can you believe it's been twenty years?" she asked.

"No, it doesn't seem like we've been married that long."

"I know, right, but it's been the best ride of my life and you've been the best husband a girl could ask for. I do dreadfully adore you, and I am most proud of you," she said before kissing his lips gently.

"I love you too, more than you will ever know."

He kissed her cheek as several knocks on their bedroom door startled them.

"Yes, Rosa," she said, as Webster walked into the bathroom and out of sight.

"Excuse me, Señora Praeliou, would you like me to make your breakfast now?" asked Rosa, her housekeeper.

"No, I think I'll take a ride this morning. I would like a hot bath drawn for me when I come back and then I'll have my breakfast," she said, tying her hair in a long ponytail on top of her head.

"You going riding?"

"Yes. I will see you when you get back. Safe travels, my love," she said, lending a quick peck of the lips to seal the deal of safely returning to her. While Webster showered, she quickly dressed and grabbed a pair of rusty brown Valentino riding boots from her closet.

The stables where her champion stallion thoroughbreds were kept was a half-mile walk from the house. Carlos, their butler, had a golf cart. Rosa used a walkie-talkie to reach him and he was at the side door waiting to whisk Diana away to the stables. Polo, Misfit, and Rags were all retired now from racing, but they had made their owner, Diana Praeliou, a very rich woman. Misfit had won the Kentucky Derby and had taken the Triple Crown. Misfit had made Diana rich beyond her wildest dreams. Rags had won four Grade One races, including the Breeders Cup Classic at Belmont Park, and he was Horse of the Year in 2004, 2005, and 2006. He retired with a record of twelve wins, nine second-place finishes, and one third-place finish. His career earnings topped $3,453,220, no cents required. She herself would have never believed it had she not known better. Polo, until he injured his left leg, had been a prize-winning racehorse. His record far outweighed that of Misfit and Rags. He took home first place at every race, and every horse show, but after he fell and suffered a fractured leg, she never raced him again. Instead, he retired to a quiet, tranquil life with her. "We might be a little broken, hey, Polo, but we're survivors, huh, boy," she'd always tell him, feeling most attached to him and most grateful for all the high times he had brought her.

It was Webster who first introduced Diana to the thrill of riding. Until then, the last creature she ever dreamed of having for a pet was a horse, but Diana loved her stallions so passionately that she cared for them personally. Even though she had stable boys to walk them, feed them, and brush them daily, she still every day was hands-on with them. For her, they were the babies she never had, and she loved each of them dearly. Some women get dogs from their husbands, Diana got thoroughbreds. Sometimes she thought she was closer to her horses than she was to her husband. All the time he spent at the hospital and at Bio One's pharmaceutical facility took up the time he would have spent being the perfect, doting husband. But Diana understood, and she gave her husband all the mental and physical support he needed to be one of the creative, genius forces behind Bio One's search for a cure to Alzheimer's. It was unbelievable, and she would have never imagined twenty years ago that her life would be this rich in luxury or love, but it was, and now her husband was receiving recognition for his contributions in medicine. His discoveries were groundbreaking. The practice of medicine had led Webster all over the world to care for the sick. And over the years he had grown into the security of having a beautiful, strong, faithful wife by his side. Not only was Diana the epitome of grace and charm, but she had a feminine quality that other women seemingly could not project. She walked into a room and effortlessly illuminated it. People were attracted to her beauty and charm, and of course most of the men in their tight-knit circle of friends secretly lusted to share her bed. They were unable to take their eyes off her, even in the presence of her husband. If he hadn't been told what a lucky man he was at least one hundred thousand times, his name wasn't Webster Praeliou. Her every move was watched, from how she held her husband's hand, to how she danced the waltz, to every bite she'd take of her liver pâte. And she commanded respect. Had she wished for others to bow as if in the presence of true royalty, then it would have been so. In the secret society of Scottsdale's who's who, Webster and Diana Praeliou were at the top of the list, invited to every event and envied by everyone who had the pleasure of being in their company. They were the social couple of the century, throwing fundraisers and donating time to raising funds for city and state officials.

Diana Praeliou could throw a barbecue in her backyard and rake in more than five hundred thousand dollars for charity. She was a mover and a shaker and she made things happen. Every year Diana threw a Christmas party in their home for all Webster's family and their friends. The guest list was over five hundred people and counting. Every name on the list was someone of great importance from the city and state politicians to the medical professionals associated with her husband's practice and every other scientist on his team from Bio One. They were all in attendance. No doubt, Webster and Diana Praeliou had the perfect life, she was the perfect wife, and he was the perfect husband. They were two souls that had joined together as man and wife in a union truly blessed by God. And in the past twenty years, there had been no man or woman who could come between them. How many women could say they were married to a neurosurgeon, a genius, a rich, handsome genius who happened to be on the cusp of a cure for Alzheimer's? Forget the money. They were rich beyond their wildest dreams, but then again, money meant nothing, they already had everything they wanted financially and materially, and most important, they had each other, and for the two of them, that was all that mattered.

Diana finished her ride with Rags, patted him down, told him what a good boy he was at least one hundred times, then called for Carlos on the walkie-talkie. Once in her bedroom, she began to undress as Rosa prepared her bath and turned on the plasma flat-screen hanging on the wall above the Jacuzzi. She put on a robe and walked into the wall-to-wall marble bathroom. She handed her robe to Rosa as Rosa held her hand and helped her sit down.

"*Bien?*" Rosa asked.

"*Si, bien,* Rosa, *gracias.*"

The Jacuzzi sat kitty-corner under a large window with a perfect, picturesque view of the Arizona desert and Camel Back Mountain. Several large saguaros, cactuses, and palo verdes lined the yard. There were scattered patches of red fairy dusters and desert willows and a few summer poppies strategically placed around the backyard. Arizona was truly the home of mother earth and all the holistic benefits of the desert were there at Diana's fingertips. At forty-two years old, she looked as if she could pass for her late twenties or early thirties.

"Señora Praeliou, will you be eating downstairs today?" asked Rosa.

"No, I'll eat on the bedroom balcony. Bring the newspaper and the mail also," she ordered before pressing a button and turning on the twenty-two-jet Jacuzzi.

Diana finished her bath and dressed in a cool tan-colored sweatsuit and white tee. Her toes were perfectly manicured, and she slipped on a pair of Bonjour Fleurette slippers and made her way to the balcony. A tray containing fresh fruit, toast, preserves, and freshly squeezed orange juice was waiting on the master bedroom balcony. She sat down, glanced at the headlines in today's *Arizona Capitol Times*, and then started to open the small pile of mail.

The envelope she held in her hand was handwritten, barely legible, foreign to her. She opened it and pulled out a folded sheet of yellow tablet paper. Small and large cut-out letters that had been pasted on the page read: "I know who you are, Daisy. Does your husband? Call this number 602-555-3773 at 4:00 P.M. today or I call Webster!"

Large letters, small letters, red letters, black letters, white letters all cut out and pasted on yellow tablet letter paper. She read it again, and again, and again as a horrible feeling of uncertainty fell on her shoulders like a heavy burden. It seemed as though someone was out there, watching her. *He called Webster by name. Oh, my God, what am I going to do?* She folded the note back up and put it back in the envelope.

"What am I going to do?"

"I so sorry, you talk to me, Señora?" asked Rosa, who was coming in to take the tray.

"Oh, my God, you startled me," said Diana. She had not realized Rosa was in the room behind her. "Rosa, please, some privacy for one moment."

"Do you need anything, Señora?"

"No, no, just a few minutes alone."

"*Si*, Señora," Rosa said, closing the bedroom door behind her.

Diana began to pace across the floor of the room. *What do they want? Why, why now, after all these years, why?* All those years of lying, pretending, and living a life that was a lie. She thought back to when she was younger, to all the mistakes of her past. She thought she had put them to rest, skeletons in a locked closet. She had paid the price and been given another chance at life. But now, all that was turning upside down and her past was here, right here in her present. *Jesus, what am I going to do?* She had no options. The bottom line was Webster could never, ever find out who she really was or any other sordid detail of her dirty, trifling life. Her secrets had to remain safe and unknown. It would ruin her marriage, ruin her life, and ruin everything. No, her secrets must never

ever be exposed. She would do whatever had to be done to keep her past life a lie. She had to. She had no other choice. It was the only way to protect her husband and to protect their perfect life.